Korean CURE-All

The sweet herbs filled the tiny hut with their fragrance. Patiently Chiun wrung poultices from cold water and placed them on Smith until his shivering stopped and his fever began to break.

His eyes flickered open. "Should have . . . should have . . ."

"Silence," Chiun said softly. "You are still in grave danger."

Smith touched his ear, grimacing at the pain. It was covered with wet, sweet-smelling silk. Chiun's kimono sleeve was torn, and Smith knew he had made the bandage with it. "Thank you," he whispered.

Chiun nodded. "It is nothing."

Smith gasped for air. "Remo?" he asked weakly.

Chiun's face was impassive. "He did not come out from the cave."

It took Smith a long time before he could gather the strength to speak again. "I changed his destiny," he said.

Chiun looked at him with an odd compassion. "No," he said. "You did not."

"CURE—"

"You do not understand the ways of Sinanju, Emperor. This is his destiny. . . ."

THE DESTROYER SERIES:

The Destroyer #49

SKIN DEEP

Warren Murphy

PINNACLE BOOKS   NEW YORK

For Eiko and Pat

DESTROYER #49: SKIN DEEP

Copyright © 1982 by Richard Sapir and Warren Murphy

An original Pinnacle Books edition, published for the first time anywhere.

First printing, July 1982

ISBN: 0-523-41559-1

Cover illustration by Hector Garrido

Printed in the United States of America

PINNACLE BOOKS, INC.
1430 Broadway
New York, New York 10018

SKIN DEEP

Chapter One

A storm was coming. Thick smoke-colored clouds gathered to the west, already rumbling with thunder. The sea, normally sparkling and calm in the key waters off the South Florida coast, now whipped frothy and gray against the hull of the U.S.S. *Andrew Jackson.*

Lieutenant Richard Caan put on his rain slicker and moved quickly to the landing strip at the stern of the ship. The dull ache that had been pounding at the back of his skull all night was charging at full gallop now. He checked the wind and spat over the side of the railing, but the taste from the night before remained in his mouth.

"You the pilot, sir?" a young ensign asked as Caan stepped briskly toward the tarpaulin-covered dual-engined jet.

"Copilot," answered Caan.

"Good enough." The young man saluted.

The ensign's crew had already seen to securing and covering the F-24. Her outline stood out sleekly beneath the fluttering tarpaulin: the needle-sharp nose, the huge wasp's wings, the streamlined bulge of the fuel tanks.

She was the most exotic plane Caan had ever flown, the most efficient fighter-bomber ever constructed. Almost always he felt a flush of pride at seeing the magnificent machine. Only a handful of men in the world knew how to fly her as yet, and Caan was one of them. But he felt no pride now.

"We've got her battened down pretty secure, sir," the ensign said. "You might want to check her for stability, though."

"Thank you, ensign," Caan said, his eyes lingering for a moment on the young man. The taste in his mouth was repugnant. It was unfamiliar to him, the taste of defeat, of violence and death and imagined hell.

It was fear.

"Yes, sir?" the ensign asked uncertainly, the high wind pinching the young man's farm-fresh features.

Caan forced himself back to composure. "That'll be all."

"Yes, sir." The young man saluted and led his small crew away.

Caan swallowed as he examined the pinnings on the plane.

There will be terrible destruction.

His head ached mercilessly. The events of the night before—a thousand years ago, it seemed now, back in the security of the Key West Naval Base—flashed before him with terrifying accuracy.

Terrible destruction . . .

It began with his awakening. With a painful jolt he had been forced out of deep sleep into a sitting position, his two arms hammer-locked behind him. A cold, black-gloved hand clamped like a vise over his mouth.

"You are one of the pilots scheduled to sail tomorrow on board the *Andrew Jackson?*" an unseen voice behind him hissed. The voice was heavily accented, guttural. The hands yanked back hard on Caan's arms. He nodded.

"I have placed a vial on your bed, beside you."

Caan's frightened gaze wandered to his lap. Next to his legs lay a small dark bottle.

"Take it with you tomorrow. There will be terrible destruction. You will not be able to stop it. When it happens, place the contents of the vial on your face and head. Do as I say, or you will die." The strong hands forced Caan's neck back sharply. "Wait for the birds. They will be your sign."

Those were the last words he heard. With a deafening crack, something came down on the back of Caan's head. A splintering pain, and then blackness.

He came to at three A.M. Staggering groggily to the door of his Quonset hut, he stood in the darkness and listened. The Key West base, disbanded in recent years, was nearly deserted except for a vestigial research team and the sleeping crew of the *Andrew Jackson*, now snoring peacefully in unaccustomed privacy. The only sounds came from night insects and the drone of the sea.

4

Birds?

Was it a dream? A crazy nightmare brought on by an attack of nerves? The next day would be Caan's first maneuvers on an aircraft carrier. Maybe the prospect of a long sea voyage just went against his grain. He doubled back to his bunk.

It was there. The vial.

He switched on the light. The sudden brightness made the pain at the back of his head shoot suddenly. He held the bottle up to the light, squinting.

Inside the amber-colored glass was clear, viscous liquid. He unscrewed the cap and sniffed. The odor made him sputter and gag. Whatever was in there was the foulest-smelling stuff he'd ever run into. He put the lid back on tightly, placed the bottle on the corner of his desk, and switched off the light. He would take it to the base commander later that morning, before they sailed.

There will be terrible destruction. . . .

The bottle glinted in the moonlight. Slowly Caan picked it up and slipped it into the breast pocket of his uniform.

"Wake up, Lieutenant. This is no place to be daydreaming."

Caan snapped to. He felt rain whipping against his skin. His trousers beneath the slicker were soaked through and freezing. "Yes, sir, Commander." he said.

"Everything in good order here? Or haven't you bothered to look?" the Commander demanded with the shrill petulance of a spoiled child.

Arlington Mills Albright, the Commander, was fairly young, but the kind of man who was accustomed to giving orders. Even if he didn't know anything about what he was ordering, Caan thought with a certain grouchiness. Albright was less qualified to fly the F-24 than he was. But he had gone to Annapolis, and was a Commander, and so was the senior pilot on the plane during the *Andrew Jackson* maneuver.

"All checked out, sir," Caan said.

"Good." Albright patted him on the shoulder patronizingly. "You turned out to be of some use to me, after all."

A huge shaft of lightning streaked eastward. "Yes, sir," Caan muttered.

Albright headed back for the shelter of the ship's interior. At the port, though, he hesitated and motioned to his copilot. "Come in out of the rain, at least," he said with a condescending smirk.

Caan obeyed. "Those sailors can take care of the ship. We'd only be in the way anyway. No one needs flyers in a storm, right?"

"I suppose not, sir."

"We might as well just sit this out over a game of gin."

"I don't play gin rummy, sir."

The Commander looked annoyed. "Well, sit down anyway," he ordered. He caught himself, and worked a tone of rich man's camaraderie into his voice. "We'll have coffee and discuss

6

the price of grain, eh?" He chuckled and patted Caan on the back again.

Caan sat. Outside, the thunder rolled. He saw Albright glance quickly out the porthole, his brow furrowed, before returning his gaze to Caan with forced friendliness. The commander busied himself for a few minutes ordering coffee from the cook on duty. When the cups were placed in front of the two men, he rubbed his hands together in a parody of cheerful enthusiasm. "Well, then. Since you're not familiar with gin, how about a rubber of bridge? Nothing like bridge, I say, to bring out a man's powers of reason."

"I don't play bridge either, sir," Caan said levelly.

Albright looked dismayed. "Oh. Then—"

"Sir, did a strange man come to your quarters last night?" he blurted.

The commander's patrician features set hard. "What made you ask that?"

"Because one came to me. He asked me if I was a pilot. There are only two of us on board, and you're senior to me." He shrugged.

There was a long silence. "Utter nonsense," the commander said at last. "Some fool's idea of a prank, no doubt."

More silence.

"Don't you think so?" Albright asked, rather nervously, Caan thought.

"No," he said quietly. "I didn't think it was a prank."

The two cups of coffee grew cold, untouched, in front of them.

7

"You did throw that stinking stuff away, didn't you?" the commander asked with a smile.

Caan shook his head. "Did you?"

"Of course," Albright said indignantly. His voice growing louder, he added, "If you think that I'm going to let some punk threaten Arlington Mills Albright for one minute—"

"I didn't think anything, sir." His headache was throbbing again. He rubbed his temples with his fingertips.

"It stands to reason you'd keep yours," Albright said, rising jerkily. "Probably tied around your neck along with a rabbit's foot for good measure. Your people have always been superstitious."

Caan looked up, his face expressionless. "Does that go with being pushy, stingy, dirty, and unfit for membership in your country club? Sir?"

"You insubordinate little Jew," Albright said with contempt, and walked out.

Caan sighed. He put his wet slicker back on and headed out into the rain.

"Jesus Christ, will you look at that!" Someone near Caan was pointing toward the western sky.

"Gotta be a twister," someone else confirmed.

"Nah, twister's got a tail on it. Or sompin'. They ain't no tail on that thing."

"But it's moving."

It's moving *this way*, Caan thought.

"Wait a second. Let's have a look-see through

8

these glasses," one of the men said, raising a pair of binoculars. He lowered them again, slowly.

"Well?"

"Damnedest thing."

"What's that?"

"It's birds."

Caan turned around sharply. *Wait for the birds. They will be your sign.* "What?"

"It's birds, sir," the seaman said, suddenly aware of Caan's presence. Caan moved toward the rail to get a better look, hanging on against the rolling of the ship.

"Gimme them glasses," one of the sailors said, snatching away the binoculars. "Can't hardly see with this rain and all."

"Goddamn *birds*, I tell you."

"What kind of birds?" an observer asked.

"I dunno. Seagulls, it looks like."

"They're the size of buzzards," the man looking through the binoculars said incredulously.

Caan placed his hand over his breast pocket. The vial lay over his thundering heart. *There will be terrible destruction.* "Clear the decks," he said, turning back toward the seamen.

"Sir, it's only some birds—"

"Clear the decks, I said!"

The sailors backed away from him. "Yes, sir," the senior one said hesitantly. Caan saw him striding toward one of the ship's officers. The officer, a lieutenant commander, cast an angry glance at Caan, barked something at the seamen, and stormed over toward the copilot.

9

"What is the idea of telling my men to clear the decks in the middle of a storm?" he raged.

"It's the birds, sir," Caan began to explain.

"Haven't you ever seen birds before? You're a pilot, for God's sake, you must have run across them once or twice."

"It's not like that, sir—"

"Look here, Lieutenant. We've got weather on our hands that's getting worse by the minute. My men can't clear the decks just because of a few birds. Is that clear?"

"You've got to believe me!" Caan shouted. "These aren't ordinary birds."

The other officer's lips tightened. "I think you'd better stick to flying planes, son."

"But—"

"That'll be all." The lieutenant commander walked away.

No one needed binoculars to see the birds now. They were giants, with six-foot wing spans and powerful bodies gliding above claws that jutted downward like gnarled trees as they reached the great ship.

"They're coming—they're coming *here*," someone shouted, too late.

"Oh, my God," Caan groaned. They were already attacking.

Through the violent rain, he saw a young man, dressed in a slicker like his own, stumble backward onto the deck. His hands flailed spastically as powerful talons swooped down, scooping out his throat with one deadly swat. Another screamed, high and keening with his last breath, as one of the creatures descended on him, picking out his eyes with its blood-stained beak.

Caan wanted to turn away, but some dreadful fascination held him. All around him was carnage and chaos and . . . *terrible destruction*, he thought, the voice inside him giddy with hysteria as he watched the birds, obscene in their size and sickly whiteness, pounce with a near-lust on their human victims.

Someone was running toward him, his head low, his big frame lunging desperately ahead. It was Albright. His eyes were pleading, his hands grasping at the rain pouring in front of him. "Caan!" he called. "The vial . . . "

The birds shrieked like banshees. Almost absently, Caan lifted the dark bottle from his pocket and stared. Was it a joke, the magic contents of the vial? Another bad dream? Beyond the vial, he saw the lumbering Albright with his hungry, twisted face and outstretched fingers.

"Give it to me!" he screamed pitifully. "Give it to me, Caan. I beg you."

And beyond him, the frantic men, blind, maimed, dying in oceans of their own blood while the monster gulls killed slowly, wantonly.

"Caan!"

The copilot stood, shocked into utter stillness, the amber bottle resting on his open palm, as the birds closed in on the commander. A flutter of white wings, one long, ghostly scream, and then Albright lay in a twisted heap of limbs and sinews, his blood mixing with the rain and washing the deck in bright splatters.

"Oh, my God," Caan said again.

11

And then they were coming for him. A squadron of shiny black eyes and red-tipped vultures' beaks, the wings beating a slow tattoo of death.

"Do something, Caan," he muttered aloud to himself as the birds drew inexorably nearer. A jagged prong of lightning illuminated the sky for an instant. In the light, he noticed his own fingers shaking with comic exaggeration as he fumbled for the cap of the vial.

Even with the high winds, he could smell the foul liquid in the bottle as he poured it onto his scalp and face. He felt a manic giggle rise from deep inside him. What if it was a joke, after all—if when he was found, dead and stinking of whatever vile concoction was in the bottle, the clean-up crews tossed coins to see who would get stuck with bagging his body? He giggled wildly until he broke, weeping, watching the birds swoop down for his inglorious final moment.

They passed him.

Behind him he heard the death screams of others, but the beating wings above him did not fold and drop and come for him. Angels' wings, he thought, seeing the flapping white feathers pass overhead.

The Angel of Death had passed him by.

He was not a religious man, not a Jew in any sense other than that he had been raised, nominally, as a Jew during his earliest years. His parents were not even practicing Jews any longer. Still, he knew of Passover, and it must have been the same then, thousands of years ago, when his ancestors eluded the cold kiss of the Angel with its dread white wings.

He fell to his knees, found a post to hang onto against the worsening wind, and prayed.

In time—how much time? . . . a moment? . . . an hour?—the din of gulls subsided, their flapping receded into the distance, and Caan shivered with the cold rain and wind against the back of his neck. Then he raised his head tentatively and gasped

Around him, in a square, stood four men. They were dressed in diving gear, their faces blackened with grease. Past them, all was silence except for the howl of the wind and the unending machine-gun fire of the pelting rain. Bodies lay everywhere, sprawled indecently, their faces open with surprise and sudden, painful death. The figure of commander Albright still lay where he had fallen, the rigid fingers still searching uselessly, his frenzied quest forever failed. Nothing lived on the *Andrew Jackson* now except for Lieutenant Richard Caan, undistinguished Navy copilot, indifferent Jew spared from death by the sheerest whim of fate, and four strange men reeking with the stench of the fluid from the amber-colored vial.

One of the four spoke. His eyes, encircled by black grease, were the palest blue, their shape narrow and serpentine. Caan recognized the voice as belonging to his visitor of the night before.

"Get in the plane," he said.

13

Chapter Two

His name was Remo, and he was swimming underwater at twenty knots, slackening off his top speed to keep pace with a school of dolphins that had temporarily adopted him.

Curious about their new playmate, they nosed him gently and chattered in a supersonic chorus as he dipped and rolled with them, dived deep and shot up for air.

It was getting dark. His excercise period was over, but he was enjoying himself with the clownish bottle noses, and besides, nothing was waiting for him back in Key West except for Chiun, who would be watching television anyway.

Reluctantly, he left the dolphins and headed back in the general direction of land. That was the basic trouble with being an assassin, he thought, as he came up for air near the beginning of Seven Mile Bridge, the only overland route into Key West. He was stuck with fish. There weren't many people for a professional killer to relate to.

There was Chiun, of course, his trainer and teacher. Chiun was the Master of Sinanju, the greatest assassin alive, but he was still an eighty-year-old man whose principal interests ran toward ancient Korean poetry, reruns of 1965 soap operas, and a terrorist Oriental news anchorwoman named Cheeta Ching. And killing people. Not exactly your scintillating after-dinner conversationalist.

Using as markers the long steel poles rooting the bridge to the ocean floor, Remo dived and swam underwater for the next half-mile. Up for air, watching the cars overhead breezing into the country's southernmost land mass, back under for another half-mile. After ten minutes he was on land, running down Roosevelt Boulevard, past the acres of shopping complexes and fast-food eateries known collectively as "New Key West," waving occasionally to honking cars filled with pretty girls, and turned onto Truman Avenue into the old town, *Cayo Hueso*, as the Spaniards first called it, with its winding tropical streets and warm kitchen smells tinged with Cuban coffee and the pungent sweetness of crawfish.

He was feeling better. His last assignment from upstairs had not gone smoothly. More lives had been lost than he'd counted on, and he had had to travel halfway around the world with an injury to his nervous system that had nearly killed him. After it was over, Remo never wanted to work again. But now, in the fragrant Florida sunlight, surrounded by an explosion of orchids and hibiscus and frangipani, he was growing stronger.

"Let's see, let's see," he mumbled as he continued to enumerate the human beings he was close to. "Chiun," he said, holding up one finger. "And . . ." He scoured his mind.

Parents couldn't count, because Remo didn't have parents, and the nuns at the orphanage where he was raised didn't count either, since he never got to know many of them well, and those who knew him did not like him. The cops at the precinct in Newark couldn't count because he was still a rookie on the force when he got bleeped out of official existence, framed for a crime he didn't commit and sentenced to die in an electric chair that didn't work. Only everyone thought it did work, and that Remo had died in it, because it had been set up that way by the sneakiest, coldest, least human individual in America. . . .

Remo held up a second finger. "Smith," he said disgustedly.

Dr. Harold W. Smith, director of Folcroft Sanitarium in Rye, New York, was Remo's second and only other link to the rest of humankind.

Folcroft was Smith's cover for what he really did, which was to employ Remo as the enforcement arm of an organization called CURE. It was a secret organization, an extra legal offshoot of the president's office. CURE's job was to control crime by functioning outside the Constitution.

Sometimes Smith worked alone, pulling out

17

information from the giant computer banks built into Folcroft and getting that information to the right people through thousands of innocuous channels—clerks who thought they were informing for the FBI, government workers who thought it was the CIA who was sending them small but helpful checks each month, reporters who thought they had a hush-hush link with the Treasury Department.

But Smith didn't always work alone. Sometimes—when somebody needed to be bumped off, to be precise—Remo worked for him.

That was the depressing part. As if killing people wasn't bad enough, Remo had to kill people for the dullest, driest, most extraordinarily boring and humorless man on the globe.

Smith had sent him to Key West three days before, to "await further instructions," as the lemon-faced New Englander had put it. Smith always talked as if he were writing memos. "Awaiting further instructions," of course, meant that Remo was going to have to cream someone pretty soon.

What a way to make a living, he thought as he sprinted past the chic boutiques on Duvall Street, past the Bull and Whistle, where the area's tough guys strutted, past the throbbing discos, where too-pretty boys displayed their wares with studied decadence to moneyed old men. The carnival midway of Old Key West was already in full swing, beckoning with its lights and music and tropical sea breezes to sailors, lovers, Caribbean blacks, college kids, local shrimpers, and sponge fishermen.

Remo went on the Mallory Dock, where the tourists had long since finished applauding the nightly sunset as if it were a Broadway production. Near the dock was Chiun's and Remo's temporary home, a quiet little Conch house, built indestructibly by local craftsmen, or "conches," and surrounded by the wild orange blossoms of massive poinciana trees.

"I'm home, Chiun," Remo said.

The frail old Oriental with tufts of white, wispy hair in patches on his head and chin sat on a mat on the floor, his almond eyes transfixed on the television, where the lizard-eyed, venom-tongued Cheeta Ching spewed out the day's misdeeds with spiteful relish.

"A naval aircraft carrier bearing the mangled bodies of 213 dead crew members, undoubtedly the victims of yet another U.S. government plot against its oppressed people, has been discovered off the coast of Florida," the newscaster said. On the wall above the television hung a color photograph of the same woman, encased in an ornate gilt frame. "More details of the Navy Death Ship tonight at eleven. Till then, this is Cheeta Ching, the voice of truth."

"Hi," Remo said, trying again for the old man's attention.

Chiun ignored him.

"It's a nice night. I thought maybe we'd go into town, look things over. We could have a good time."

"Silence, brainless one," Chiun said, still staring fixedly at the television.

Remo sighed. It occurred to him that if he had

19

known he was going to have to spend his life with only two people, and one of them was going to be an eighty-year-old Korean assassin and the other was going to be Harold W. Smith, he would have stayed on at the orphanage.

A thousand miles away, in Washington, D.C., a score of top U.S. government officials sat in darkness as they watched slides depicting the gory aftermath of the massacre aboard the U.S.S. *Andrew Jackson.*

"This is typical of the sort of damage in-flicted," said a uniformed officer who had been introduced as a forensic scientist. He waved a pointer over a slide showing a man with no eyes and a gaping hole in the middle of his neck. "Can we have a closeup of this, please?" he asked politely.

The projector clicked, and the festering neck wound sprang into bloody detail. Somebody swore softly.

"Of course, these bodies weren't found until some three days after the deaths occurred, so a certain amount of decomposition had set in. Still, you see the general idea. Next."

The following slide showed the deck of the ship, littered with slaughtered bodies and tinged with the rusty-brown remains of a sea of blood.

"Good Lord," someone said.

The slides flashed one after the other. Dead men lying in macabre repose in their bunks, in the mess hall, frozen in position in the latrine, in the engine room, charred and blackened from the heat of the furnaces, keeled over at the controls on the bridge. "This is how the ship was found," the medical examiner continued. "No one alive on board, anywhere."

"Wasn't there an alarm sent, an April-day or something?" a man in an impeccably tailored suit asked from the darkness. He was the Secretary of Defense of the United States.

"No Mayday, sir," a gruff voice belonging to a vice-admiral answered.

"Weren't they in radio contact with somebody?"

"No, sir. They were on top-secret maneuvers to try out the sea-landing capability of the F-24. It's a new bomber designed to fly without radar detection—"

"I know about the F-24," the secretary said drily. "I'm paying for it. I pay for everything around here. The stealth bomber. What's that got to do with it?"

The vice-admiral hemmed and hawed. "Actually, quite a bit, sir. You see—" He stammered, cleared his throat, then tried another tack. "To get back to the maneuvers, sir. Since the stealth bomber was to be launched, the ship was under orders to avoid radio contact for forty-eight hours unless the F-24 was detected by radar. That would have meant the bomber had failed, and radio contact would have confirmed its location. Since we didn't hear from the *Andrew Jackson*, we assumed the maneuvers were a success."

"A success," the secretary growled. "It's only a success if it's free. How did you eventually find the ship, anyway?"

"A cruise ship heading back from the Caribbean found her by accident, sir."

"A cruise ship!" the secretary bellowed. "Swell. All we need is publicity and a media circus."

"There's no reason to panic," the medical examiner said hastily. "After all, those men on board didn't die of any disease. No one's going to catch anything from them."

"Fine. Wonderful. There's no reason to panic, none at all. Two hundred and fourteen well-trained sailors on secret maneuvers with the most powerful bomber ever invented are murdered off the coast of Florida, that's all. What the hell do you mean there's no reason for panic?" he yelled. "The president's going to hang me."

"Two hundred and thirteen men, sir," the medical examiner corrected diffidently. "One was missing. We presume he must have been washed overboard. From the looks of things, they ran into some bad weather."

"Who was it? An officer?"

"Yes, sir," the vice-admiral said. "A Lieutenant Richard Caan. The copilot of the F-24."

"Well, at least we save some life insurance," the secretary said. "Anything else?"

"We do have more slides, sir," the medical examiner said.

"Hang the slides. Anything else?"

The vice-admiral coughed into his fist. "Well, yes, sir. We were coming to that. One piece of machinery was also missing."

"Which?" the secretary asked, a spark of alarm already showing in his eyes. "How much did it cost?"

The vice-admiral took a deep breath. "The F-24, sir. The stealth bomber."

A rumble rose from the small crowd.

The secretary stood up slowly. Even in the dark, every man in the room could see the color drain from his face. "It is clear that the United States Navy has been incapable of containing this problem," he said slowly and quietly. "I had better inform the president." He swept over the room with a gesture. "Proceed with the meeting, gentlemen. Do not let me keep you from your slides." He turned briskly and walked out of the room.

From the back row of seats, another man rose inconspicuously. He was an ordinary, dull-looking middle-aged man with graying hair, steel-rimmed spectacles, a three-piece gray suit, an attaché case, and a pinched, lemony expression. He, too, left the meeting.

In the corridor, he turned left, walked two doors down, and entered a small room containing a smaller cubicle constructed of plexiglass and guaranteed to be bug-free.

He locked the door to the small room, stepped into the plexiglass cubicle, opened his attaché case containing a small red computer-powered telephone, and waited. Harold W. Smith was expecting a call from the President of the United States.

He checked his watch. The call wouldn't

come for another twenty minutes, at least, but he had no need to watch more of the grisly pictures in the meeting room. He had known there would be trouble, ever since a report two months before concerning a "lost" cargo ship—another casualty of the Bermuda Triangle, according to the press. But Smith knew from several clandestine sources that the ship hadn't been lost until the Navy sank it, quietly disposing of the mutilated bodies on board when no answer to the riddle of the massacre could be found.

The Navy, the Coast Guard, the Army, the Air Force. They had all tried. They had all failed. That was why the president had asked Harold W. Smith to Washington, to the top-level briefing on the *Andrew Jackson* enigma, to the tiny plexiglass room with no listening devices.

The phone rang. "Yes, Mr. President," Smith said.

The voice at the other end was weary. "The F-24 is missing," the president said.

"Yes, sir."

The deep voice spoke deliberately. "You know, of course, about the summit meeting scheduled for this week in New York City?"

"I do," Smith said.

"The Soviet premier will have heard about the incident on board the *Andrew Jackson* and the missing stealth bomber by then."

"It cannot be avoided," Smith said.

The president spoke softly. "The stealth is the only thing that's making these bastards want to talk seriously about reducing forces. With it gone, we won't have any bargaining position at all. We have to get it back."

"My man is in position in Key West," Smith said. "He's prepared to take action immediately."

"How's that?" the president asked, shocked.

"He arrived five hours after the ship was discovered."

"But the briefing today was the first disclosure of the incident, even to top-security-cleared personnel. How did you know about it?"

There was a long pause. "Will that be all, sir?" Smith asked.

The president sighed. "One man . . . "

"Good day, sir," Smith said, and hung up.

It had just been a matter of time, Smith knew, before CURE would be called in. That was why he had placed Remo in Key West at the first rumblings of the *Andrew Jackson* fiasco. He replaced the phone in his briefcase, locked it, left the plexiglass-enclosed room, and walked quickly into the street, to a pay phone where he began the long routing codes that would eventually connect him securely with his human weapon.

Remo Williams. The Destroyer.

Just a matter of time.

That time had come.

Chapter Three

The small rowboat slid noiselessly through the blue water. Remo's arms ached. He had been rowing for more than twelve hours, since before dawn, steering the tiny craft in ever-widening circles from the point where the *Andrew Jackson* had been sighted.

"This is useless," he said, throwing down the oars. "That ship drifted for three days before it was found. We don't even know what we're looking for. There must be thousands of islands in the Florida Keys."

"There," Chiun said, pointing in the distance to a cluster of postage-stamp-sized islands. The tuft of white hair on top of the old Oriental's head fluttered in the breeze. "Take us to that island. The one with the concealed path."

Remo looked to the cluster, then back at Chiun sitting like a dowager in the back of the boat. "There's no concealed path, Little Father," Remo said, suppressing a smile. "These islands have never been inhabited."

"Thus said Marco Polo to the Master Hun Tup when they approached China," Chiun snapped. "Stop your arrogant prattling and drive us to the island."

Remo turned the boat toward the islands. "A Master of Sinanju was with Marco Polo?" he asked.

"One of the finest. You think the white man could have found anything by himself? Had Hun Tup not persisted, the expedition would have ended up on the Arctic subcontinent."

"No egg rolls for the crew, I guess."

"Polo would have been like that crazed Columbus, who claimed that your country was India. How could it be India without filth and curry and plague?"

"But Columbus didn't have a Master of Sinanju on board," Remo said, smiling.

"He did, unfortunately. Ko Wat, the Misdirected, was with him. A minor blemish on the glorious House of Sinanju. Halt," he said, pointing. "Do you see?"

As they neared the small island, Remo narrowed the focus of his eyes until he seemed to be looking through high-powered field glasses. In the fading light he saw cleverly concealed traces of human existence: broken twigs, a sweep across the sand to cover footprints, a dead tree covering what looked like a narrow path.

"You were right," Remo said.

"And you were wrong. As usual." Chiun grinned. "As usual, heh, heh."

28

They moored the boat. A flock of fat white gulls settled lazily along the shoreline.

"Look at the size of these birds," Remo said. He felt an uncomfortable turn in his stomach when they were joined by still more seagulls, pecking idly at the ground, their black dolls' eyes never leaving the two men. "Something's funny about these birds," Remo insisted.

But Chiun was standing completely still, gazing at the bushes farther inland. "Silence," he said softly. "We are being watched."

A twig broke. Instantly Remo's attention riveted on the bushes. His muscles tensed and then relaxed, ready for the inevitable attack. Then, with a piercing yell, it came, like a vision from Hades.

There was only one man, and he was no more than a boy, judging from the awkwardness of his movements. He was squat, with the stocky, long-torsoed build of an Oriental, and he was naked except for a loincloth against his sun-darkened skin. His hair, coarse and straight and black, stood up from his head in stiff peaks. In his right hand he held a club. His left was a gnarled stump, with four fingers missing.

These were the things Remo saw first as the strange attacker leaped a foot above the tops of the bushes, screaming and wild-eyed. But a split second later, Remo no longer saw the intruder as a person. All he remembered after that moment was a face, a face so frightening and grotesque that everything else about the man became secondary.

Remo's breath caught at the sight. He ducked and spun to begin his attack, but was knocked out of the way by a tremendous force out of nowhere. It was Chiun.

"Hold," Chiun called, his yellow robe still billowing from his inexplicable assault on Remo.

"What'd you do that for?" Remo asked as in front of him the boy with the disfigured face stood unmoving, his unsightly features twisted in bewilderment.

Now Remo got a better look at him. He was an Oriental, but only vaguely so. Maybe Polynesian, Remo thought, although the scars and lesions on his skin all but obliterated his natural appearance. He was covered with sores, seeping with clear liquid, and one eyelid was swollen to half-mast, revealing the blackened remains of a dead eye beneath.

"I am the Master of Sinanju," Chiun said. "This is my son. Tell your chief we are come."

The boy's pustule-encrusted mouth opened. He dropped the club from his hand as if it were a foul thing. Then, to Remo's amazement, he emitted a small cry and fell to his knees before Chiun.

The old man touched his head. "Go," he said gently. "We will wait here."

The boy stood up, bowed again, and scurried back into the underbrush.

Remo followed him with his eyes for a few moments. When the monstrous-looking boy had disappeared into the thick jungle greenery, Remo turned to Chiun. "What was that about?" he

30

asked, rubbing the spot on his arm where Chiun had pushed him out of the boy's way. "Do you know him?"

The old man looked sadly into the brush. "He is a leper," he said. "He knows me."

Chapter Four

The birds were thick as snowdrifts around them.

"A leper?"

Chiun nodded. "And a Hawaiian. He is probably from the colony at Molokai, but I must see the rest of the tribe before I can be sure."

"Wait. Hold on," Remo said. "What is this about lepers? What do you know about lepers, anyway? And you've never even been to Hawaii. You told me that yourself once."

"One sand pit is like another," Chiun said. "But all Masters of Sinanju know of the lepers of Molokai. And they know us. Sit. I will tell you of the Decree of the great Master Hun Tup." He motioned toward a fallen tree.

"Hun Tup? Wasn't he the guy you said went to China with Marco Polo?"

Chiun beamed. "You remember well, for a white thing."

Remo grimaced. "The story," he said. "Can the insults."

"Long, long ago," Chiun began, using the

33

mystic storyteller's voice that meant he was settling into one of his windier legends, "the people of my village of Sinanju in Korea were so poor, and their catch from the ocean so meager, that they were forced to conserve rations by sending their babies back to the sea."

"Yeah, yeah, I know that part about drowning the babies. What about Wing Tip?"

"Hun Tup," Chiun corrected. "I am coming to him. Do not interrupt. You have made me lose my place." His voice shifted back into the storyteller's whisper. "Long, long ago . . ."

"*I know*, Chiun. They sent their babies back to the sea, and so the first Master of Sinanju had to rent himself out as an assassin to the highest bidder and send his paychecks back to the village, which is what every Master since has been doing."

Chiun fixed him with an angry, unblinking stare. "These legends are better when told properly," he said.

"Sorry. I just wanted you to get to the part about Marco Polo."

"A nobody," Chiun said. "A drunk. A meat-eating sailor with a nagging wife and a houseful of squealing white children. It was no wonder he wanted to go to China. It just surprised me he did not try to reach the moon."

"Was Hun Tup working for Marco Polo?" Remo asked, trying to steer Chiun back to the subject. "I mean, was he a bodyguard or something?"

"Really, Remo. Now, that is an insult. The Master of Sinanju does not work as a body-

34

guard. This is work for thugs, beasts. Even a white man can be a bodyguard. Perhaps even you could."

"Just asking," Remo said.

"Hun Tup went along on the expedition as the esteemed guest of Marco Polo and his sponsor, a powerful ruler of Venice, in whose service the Master had performed many valuable deeds. As no one in Europe knew where China—or, as it was then known, Cathay—was, Hun Tup agreed to show Marco Polo the way in exchange for carrying the Master's trunks of tribute from the Venetian ruler. There was much tribute. Emeralds, diamonds, fine rubies. All were to be delivered to Sinanju along with Hun Tup once China was 'discovered.' By Marco Polo, that is. The Koreans had discovered it long before."

"Hmmm," Remo agreed. "The Japanese, too, I guess."

Chiun's eyes narrowed into flinty hazel slits. "They don't count," he said.

"Okay, so Hun Tup led Marco Polo to China, and then Marco took the Master and his tribute from Italy back to Sinanju, and everybody lived happily ever after, right?"

"Wrong. When they reached China, the Europeans were greeted by the Mongol conqueror Kublai Khan himself. This upstart appeared to be a kind and generous man, sharing with the explorers the secrets of gunpowder and silk. Polo himself was having such a wonderful time that he stayed in Peking for twenty-four years. He was white. It probably took that long for him to get over his shock at seeing people who bathed."

"Long time to wait for a ride home," Remo admitted.

"It was worse than that. For despite their warm welcome at the Chinese court, Hun Tup knew the Emperor Kublai Khan to be a deceitful, lying thief—a man of no honor and in whom the truth was not to be found."

"What'd he do that was so terrible?"

"Him? Nothing. But his ancestor, Genghis Khan, once used the services of a previous Master of Sinanju, and weighted his tribute chest with bricks at the bottom to lessen the payment. The descendants of such a man are not to be trusted," Chiun said with an air of injured dignity. "Therefore, Hun Tup stole away in the night with his heavy tribute, before the Chinese emperor could take it and deprive the village of Sinanju of its lifeblood."

"Hun Tup sounds pretty paranoid," Remo said.

"He was correct," Chiun snapped. "Kublai Khan's soldiers followed him, as he had feared, seeking to rob the Master of his riches. Deep in the hills of China, they ambushed him. Hun Tup sent them all into the Void, of course, but he himself was left with wounds which the fetid Chinese air, combined with the Master's weakness from the long journey, did nothing to cure.

"At last he found himself near a swamp, weary and with the knowledge of death close to his heart. He dropped the chest of tribute he had carried on his back for many days, certain

36

that he would never live to see again his beloved shores of Sinanju."

"What happened?" Remo asked, getting caught up in the story. "Did he die?"

"Nearly. He was found by a tribe of lepers who had been driven out of their communities and forced to live near the swamp. The lepers nursed him back to health, protected him and, when he was well, sent an escort of two of their number to carry the tribute back to Sinanju.

"Once back in his village, Hun Tup, who was in his tenth decade, charged his successor to move the lepers to a dry and comfortable place, away from the filth and stink of the Chinese swamp. Before he died in his one hundred and fourteenth year, after the lepers had all migrated to the island of Molokai in Hawaii, he decreed that all subsequent Masters were forbidden to kill the Molokai lepers, for by their kindness was the village of Sinanju spared a terrible fate."

Remo smiled. "Nice, Chiun," he said. "Really."

The old man flushed with pride. "There has been much beautiful Ung poetry written about Hun Tup the Grateful." Closing his eyes, Chiun swayed as he chanted Korean verses in a tuneless singsong.

"The only thing is, this is Florida. What are the Molokai lepers doing here?"

Chiun shrugged. "One cannot know the answers to all things at once. The boy will tell his chief about us. We will be brought to their village. Watch and listen. All will be made clear in time."

"Wish they'd hurry up," Remo said, but Chiun was chanting again. Remo looked around at the tropical isle. Except for the quiet menace of the birds, it was as close to heaven as he'd ever seen. White and purple orchids, beaded with droplets of water from the frequent rains, hung delicately near banana trees with their pendulous burdens of fruit, and the ground was covered with the fragrant boughs of . . .

Boughs? He looked again. The entire forest floor seemed to be strewn with broken twigs and leafy branches. He swept a small area clear. Beneath the sand was something hard and smooth . . . and *black*.

"Tar," he whispered. "Chiun, come look at this." The old Oriental stopped his singing and followed Remo into the forest. "This is macadam," Remo said, "it's a road."

A few birds came along, their talons clack-clacking against the surface. "What I can't understand is, why would anyone build a road that leads directly into the ocean?"

Chiun was looking up, toward the thick upper growth of leaves on the trees. Too thick, Remo thought.

"Notice the pattern of the branches at the tops of the trees," Chiun said.

Remo did. The configuration of the leaves was somehow out of place, the branches too thick. Then he saw it. A gleaming stump of white tree trunk, very high up, nearly—but not quite—connecting with the branches overhead. He widened his pupils to see farther into the dense forest. There were more trees in the same odd condition, their tops sawn off twenty feet above ground. *All* of the trees lining the artfully concealed road had been cut.

Picking up a rock, Remo aimed it at a high branch running directly across the roadway beneath. The rock struck. The branch fell to the road with a crash. Remo walked over to the felled branch to examine it. Its base, like the tops of the trees along the roadway, had been cut cleanly. Overhead, he saw the patch of sky the branch had obscured when in place.

In place. That was it. "These trees are here for camouflage," he said.

"Exactly," Chiun agreed. "Someone worked very carefully to conceal this road."

"It's no road, Chiun." Remo swished away another section of leaves and twigs of covering the sticky pavement. "This is an airstrip. If my guess is right, the missing F-24 is somewhere right on this island."

He was exploring deeper into the forest when the dim shape of a human figure came into view out of the jungle mist. Remo stood still, nearly mesmerized by the sensual, rhythmic walk of the girl. She was graceful and slim and moved with an inner stillness and dignity rare in young women. Her black waist-length hair swayed behind her as she walked, her legs as strong and muscled as the flanks of a jungle animal.

Now brace yourself, Remo thought, anticipating the wasted face that would inevitably go with the perfect body.

He blinked when he saw it. The Polynesian

face was flawless. Her complexion was creamy and sun-bronzed, setting off two wing-shaped dark eyes that twinkled with intelligence above the high, angular planes of her cheekbones. Below them rested a straight nose with slightly flaring nostrils and a full-lipped mouth naturally tinted the pink-red of good health.

"I am Ana," the girl said, warmly but not smiling. She turned to Chiun and bowed her head respectfully. "If you will follow me, Master, I will take you to our village."

Chiun watched her but did not speak. She turned and retraced her path through the forest. As the three of them walked noiselessly over the underbrush, Remo took another look at the concealed and apparently new macadam surface.

"Excuse me," he said, The girl stopped. "Do you know when that airstrip was built? And who built it?"

The girl's eyes seemed to glaze. She spoke softly. "No one," she said enigmatically. "No airstrip. No airplanes."

"Yes, there is. I saw it," Remo persisted. "Right over there . . ."

"No airstrip," Ana repeated, and moved on.

Remo sighed and followed her. She led them through a jungle paradise of lush flowering greenery and spills of cascading water. Above, against the clear blue sky, magnificent parrots and cockatoos screeched and soared, showing off rainbows of iridescent color.

"What is that noise?" Chiun asked. Remo listened. A muted roar was coming from the east.

"It is the sound from the place of perfection," Ana said. "Would you like to see it?"

Chiun nodded. The girl veered away from the small path and took them uphill through some dense growth as the noise grew louder. When at last they emerged, they were a few hundred feet from a breathtaking waterfall. The cliff where it orginated was of tremendous height, seeming to jut straight out of the sky, and the torrent of water spilling over it crashed like thunder onto huge boulders below.

"The fall is nearly two hundred feet," the girl said.

Chiun smiled. "Beautiful," he said.

The girl's voluptuous lips turned upward at pleasing the old Oriental. "Yes," she said. "Come. My brother, Timu, is waiting in the valley. He is the head of our village."

She escorted them back onto the narrow path, and they walked downhill until they could see the thatched roofs and smoking fires from a small settlement ahead, in a clearing past the last stand of trees.

"Are you sure these people are lepers?" Remo whispered to Chiun in Korean. "I mean, the girl looks all right. Better than all right. She's gorgeous. Maybe they're just a bunch of cultists or something. . . ."

But as they entered the clearing, Remo saw for himself that Chiun had been right. Women with babies, squatting over their cooking pots, young boys playing in the open, a cluster of old men arguing with one another—all stopped whatever they were doing when the strangers entered.

And all, down to the smallest child, were ravaged and mutilated with disease.

The girl took a few steps away from Remo and Chiun, as if to position herself apart from them and with the disfigured members of her tribe. Oddly, the villagers themselves backed away when she neared them, mothers pulling their young behind them, but Ana did not appear to notice. She opened her arms wide to Remo and Chiun in the classic gesture of hospitality. But when she spoke, there was a terrible irony in her words.

"This is our home," she said. "Welcome to the Valley of the Damned."

Chapter Five

Three men stood by a hut near the center of the village. Their bodies were covered with oozing lesions, but the young man in the middle was tall and fierce looking, somehow majestic in his corroded ugliness. He spoke.

"I am Timu, chief of my people. We welcome you and your honored son, O Master of Sinanju."

"I am Chiun." The old Oriental approached the chief with a small bow. Timu returned it, then looked inquiringly at Remo.

"Remo. Nice place you've got here," Remo said, trying to avoid staring at the disintegrating faces of the lepers.

"Your son is not accustomed to viewing our sickness," Timu said, with a trace of humor.

"He is not accustomed to acting civilized," Chiun said, tossing a beady glance toward Remo. He added, whispering, "He is white." The chief nodded sagely. "I am honored that you have remembered my ancestor, Hun Tup," Chiun said.

"We do not forget those who have befriended us," Timu said. "The fellowship of suffering has kept our legends alive. The kindness of the Master Hun Tup in delivering my people from the swamps of China to the beautiful land of Molokai will be remembered forever. It was our Promised Land. On Molokai, there were fine clinics and doctors who helped us to lead good, long lives."

Remo was puzzled. He looked at the grass huts hiding the dying, their lingering coughs from the disease's damage to their lungs ringing despairingly through the still air. There was no hospital or clinic in sight. Small children walked around with limbs already decayed or amputated.

"Excuse me," he said politely, "but if Molokai had everything you needed, why are you all here, where there's nothing to help you? There isn't even a doctor here."

The chief exchanged looks with his two cronies. Haltingly he said, "There is a doctor here. Also a—a medical facility." As he spoke, the two old men flanking him stared at the ground. Timu bowed to Chiun again. "Thank you, honored Master, for your visit. But I must now ask you to leave, before you are in danger of contracting our disease."

Chiun smiled. "You wish us to leave, but not because of your sickness. Even Hun Tup, in the thirteenth century, knew that leprosy is not contagious by air. It can only be passed along through an open wound. We are in no danger from you."

Timu looked abashed. "Forgive me, O Master. I should have known you were the wisest of men. But still, you must leave. There is danger here. Not from us. But danger."

"The birds," Remo said.

A low chatter rose from the villagers. "No birds," Timu said, his eyes hard.

"They're everywhere," Remo continued. "Huge white seagulls. I've never seen anything—"

"No birds!" Timu snapped, cutting off the discussion. He closed his eyes and sighed. "Please go," he said quietly. "Go before you learn too much. The Valley of the Damned is no place for the Master of Sinanju. Quickly, before the sun sets. It is for your own good."

Chiun laid a hand on the chief's shoulder. "We will stay," he said. "We will eat with you. We will spend the night here. Tomorrow we go."

A stricken silence settled over the village. "Wait a minute," Remo said in Korean. "Maybe we'd be better off in the hills. That way, if anything goes on—"

"We stay here," Chiun said stubbornly.

Ana, the girl who had brought them to the village, stepped forward. "I am not a leper. I will serve you your meals myself. Afterward, you may have my hut to sleep in. You will be safe," she said to Remo with disdain.

Toward nightfall they dined on fruit with the entire village, gathered in the clearing. The lepers danced, if haltingly, for their visitors, and sang ancient songs, and recounted old legends for the benefit of their new friends. Amid the music and festivities, Remo was ashamed of the revulsion he had first felt for the brave tribe.

Ana must have sensed it. While the villagers were clapping and singing, she clasped his hand briefly. "You understand already," she said.

Timu shot her a terrible look, and she quickly withdrew her hand. "Leave us," the chief ordered. In a moment she was gone, disappeared into the brush.

"Why'd you send her away?" Remo asked. "She wasn't doing anything."

"My sister is a strange girl," the chief said almost apologetically. "Smart. She completed a year of medical school before joining us in our colony. She has been of great assistance to us. But do not touch her." His eyes were fearful and desperate.

"I wasn't going to take her away."

"There are things I cannot explain. But I warn you, do not befriend Ana. Do not go near her. Never. Do you understand?"

Remo took a quick look over his shoulder to the jungle, now quiet, where the girl had run, then said, "Shove it."

"Silence, Remo," Chiun said. "Their ways are not your ways."

"I just wish I knew what the hell was going on in this place," Remo muttered.

Suddenly the dancers disbanded in a frenzy. Someone pointed toward a high cluster of rocks forming a dome in the distance. Screams and hushed warnings rose up from the villagers as they scrambled to their feet, spilling the sweet fruit on the ground. Some ran into the rain forest. Others took shelter in their rough huts.

Instinctively Remo whirled around to see on all sides.

"In here," Timu commanded, gesturing toward his hut. Chiun was already being ushered inside.

"Do as he says," Chiun hissed over his shoulder. "Now, before you are seen."

From inside the hut, they watched a double line of six white soldiers goose-stepping in a worn path from the thick bushes near the giant rock cluster.

"Who are they?" Remo whispered.

Timu didn't answer. The corners of his mouth curled downward in sadness and helpless rage. He turned his back and stood, his muscles taut, facing the rear wall of the hut.

Outside, the out-of-place white soldiers marched directly to a small dwelling. A woman knelt at the doorway, her hands wrung together, tears streaming down her face as she begged the soldiers to leave. One of them shoved her out of the way with the heel of his boot and sent her sprawling into the dirt.

All six went into the hut. When they emerged, they were dragging with them an old man with half a face and one leg amputated at the knee. The old man moaned in pain. The woman lying in the dirt righted herself to her knees and screamed after them, "Let him die in peace, I beg you!"

Remo started out of the hut, but Chiun caught his arm and restrained him.

The soldiers rushed on, into the bushes and toward the high-domed rocks. Then all was silence again except for the sobs of the woman. Some villagers walked cautiously out of their huts and led her away, trying to lend comfort. Others picked up the debris of the ruined feast. Most remained hidden in their huts.

Timu moved slowly into the clearing and breathed deeply, as if to stop himself from crying aloud. He raised his face to the evening sky, already beginning to dot with the sparks of southern stars. After a few moments, he addressed himself with dignity to Chiun and Remo.

"I am sorry you had to witness this," he said. "It was for this reason I asked you to leave before sunset. These things . . ." His voice caught, but he went on. ". . . Happen here sometimes in the evenings."

"Yeah?" said Remo. "What exactly happens here in the evenings? Where did they take the old man?"

"To the clinic," a woman's voice behind him answered bitterly. It was Ana.

Timu spoke. "I told you to go."

"Brother, these are my people too," the girl pleaded. "Day after day, these monsters come to take us—to the *clinic*." She spat out the word. "That's a joke. No leper dies of leprosy on this island. It's murder, Timu. They're going to kill us, all of us—"

The chief slapped her. "You have said too much, Ana," he said, obviously struggling to control a deep fury. "Take our visitors to your hut and then begone. Do not return until to-morrow when we are again alone."

Rubbing the red spot on her cheek where Timu had struck her, the girl nodded to Remo and Chiun to follow her, then walked behind the chief's hut toward the back of the village.

"I think it's time we got some answers around here," Remo said to Chiun.

"I think it's time we did what the chief requests until we have reason to do something else," Chiun said.

"And that old man that got dragged away? He's not a reason?" said Remo.

"If you were interested in the old man, he would be a reason. But you are interested in other things," Chiun said. "Behave yourself."

The young woman was ten yards ahead of them, marching along resolutely. As they approached a small hut set far away from the other dwellings, she stopped and pointed inside. Remo stepped alongside her and touched her arm. She flinched, as if his hand were red hot.

"Don't," she said, her voice at near-panic pitch.

"I'm sorry," Remo said. "I only wanted to tell you that we'd prefer to sleep outside. I don't want to put you out of your home."

"It is my brother's wish," she said evenly.

"Where will you stay?"

She looked toward the cliffs in the center of the island. "I have a place."

Chapter Six

The jungle chattered to life at night, buzzing with the drone of insects and the calls of the night birds. In its midst, silent as a stone, the village rested.

Chiun sat in full lotus in the girl's tidy, isolated hut, facing the wall. Remo lay on a grass mat, his eyes wide open and staring at the uneven thatching of the roof.

"There's nothing here I understand," he said. "First there's a shipload of dead sailors and a missing plane. Then there's a concealed airstrip. So far, so good. Probably some connection there. But what do lepers have to do with the stealth bomber?"

He waited for an answer from Chiun, got none, and went on: "And the birds. Nobody talks about the birds. They freak out if you even mention birds around here. And then, out of the jungle, we've got a bunch of blond commandos, and they grab an old guy with maybe a month, tops, to live, and disappear with him

52

into a pile of rocks. *Rocks*, Chiun I saw them come out of the freaking boulders. Now, what's that all about?"

Again the old Oriental was silent.

"And the girl. There's a nut case for you. A perfectly healthy, beautiful girl who can't stand to be touched. A girl who lives with lepers . . ."

He pondered for a moment. The girl. She was really the part that didn't fit in. He supposed she could be on the island to give what help she could to her brother and his people, except that the lepers never came near her. Even her hut was a distance from the rest of the village. And Timu had warned—no, more than warned, commanded—Remo to stay away from her. It was as if *she* were the leper.

And she had said *murder*. "It's murder. . . . They're going to kill all of us."

Who were "they?" Why were they going to kill anybody?

"The *girl*," Remo said, sitting bolt upright.

Chiun whirled to his feet with a snort. "What is wrong with you?" he screeched. "Do you not see I am trying to sleep?"

"You were sitting up."

"I have to sprawl like a dead squirrel in the street to sleep?" Chiun demanded. "I am not a white man."

"You mean you didn't hear anything I said?"

"I heard enough to wake up, fool."

Remo paced. "It's the girl. She's the key. I know it."

"You know how to make noise, O loud-mouthed one."

"I've got to talk to her. I can't let this just drag on," Remo said.

"Apparently, you have to talk to anyone. Even sleeping persons."

"Sorry, Chiun. Go back to sleep."

"Thank you. Most gracious." He turned his back and floated to his mat again.

This time Remo listened for the old man's breathing. When it was deep and even, he stepped silently out of the hut into the jungle night.

He guessed where she would be. Stalking noiselessly through the thick brush, he climbed up the craggy hills toward the cliffs, guided by the sound of the waterfall. When the roar was at its peak, when Remo stood at the top of the great white cascade shrouded in mist and darkness, he saw her.

Ana slept a short distance from the crest of the fall, beneath the spread of an acacia tree. In the moonlight, she looked like a jungle flower— delicate, wild, painfully beautiful.

Remo knelt beside her. "Ana," he said softly.

The girl awoke with a soft flutter of dark lashes. She looked at him, momentarily puzzled, then smiled. "Hello," she said.

He took pains not to come too near, remembering her recoil from his touch. "I hope I'm not frightening you," he said.

"You're not. I'm not afraid. I couldn't help what happened . . . before."

Remo nodded, although he didn't understand. He just wanted to take her along gently, easily, to draw out what he could from her.

"Ana, I need to know some things about this place—the island, the valley. Will you help me?"

Her smile vanished. She lowered her eyes.

"Maybe I can do something," Remo offered. "No one seems very happy here."

She raised her head, and Remo saw tears in her eyes. "There can be no happiness here," she said. "This is not our home. This is only our place of death." She began to sob.

Remo watched her for a moment. He didn't want to touch her and scare her. Tentatively, he held out his hand. To his surprise, the girl took it. She laughed bitterly through her tears. "You are not afraid of me, either, are you?"

"No," he said with some surprise. "Should I be?"

She withdrew her hand. "You don't know?" She took in the look of bewilderment on his face and answered her own question. "You really don't know anything about this place, do you?"

"That's why I came to you," Remo said. "I want you to explain some things to me. The airstrip, the birds—"

She turned away sharply. Remo took her chin in his hand and brought her back to face him. "The birds," he repeated. When she didn't volunteer, he went on. "Also those soldiers who came out of nowhere."

"They were from the clinic," she said dully.

"What clinic? I didn't see anything like a hospital here."

"In the rocks. Underground. The clin—the ... the ..."

She clasped both hands to her head, her features contorted in pain, her knees pulled into her chest.

"What's the matter?" Remo asked. He put an arm around her shoulders.

"No. Oh, no, please ..."

"Lie down," he said, trying to press her gently to the ground.

"Help me. Please help me. He's killing me," she gasped, her fingers reaching desperately for Remo.

"Who? For God's sake, Ana, tell me who!"

She wound her arms tightly around his neck. "Don't let it happen," she whispered, her eyes round and frightened. He held her. "Don't let it ... don't let ..."

Then she screamed, a wild, tortured cry. "Zoran!"

She wriggled out of his arms with surprising strength. "Zoran!" she called again. She looked back once at Remo with no trace of recognition on her face, as if he had just appeared from another planet. Then she raced away toward the village and the high-domed cluster of rocks beyond, repeating the strange name.

"Zoran!" It echoed across the gorge in her wake.

Remo looked down at his hands. They were still outstretched from her embrace.

He knew from the sounds all around him that the village had awakened and come to him. The chief, Timu, was the first to appear.

56

"You have disobeyed me," he said.

"I just wanted to talk to her," Remo explained.

"You were not to go near her. It was for your own safety. Now you have put yourself, the Master Chiun, and all my people in terrible danger."

"How?" Remo asked.

From the brush, Chiun's yellow robe flashed in the moonlight. In a moment he stood beside the chief, his parchment face wrinkled with annoyance.

Dawn was beginning to seep through the raintrees, turning the mist from the waterfall into swirling rainbows. Timu broke the eerie silence among the gathering of men.

"You must leave quickly," he said to Chiun. "Take the white boy away—far away—before it is too late."

"Too late for what?" Remo asked.

Timu still addressed himself to Chiun. "Forgive my sister, Master. She cannot help herself. Ana does not have control of her own mind. Your son should not have spoken with her. He was warned."

"But where did she go? What happened to her?" Remo asked.

Timu kicked a stone on the ground. "She has gone to Zoran," he said, the anger visible in his muscles.

"Ah," Chiun said. "The name the girl was calling. What is this Zoran?"

"He is a man," Timu said. "And more than a

57

man. Zoran is he who controls all things. The threads of our lives are spun by Zoran. It is Zoran who measures the length of that thread. And Zoran cuts it at his whim."

"I see," said Remo, who didn't see at all. "Where's this Zoran come from?"

"From hell," Timu answered vehemently. "He is the devil, with the devil's power."

"The birds belong to Zoran, don't they?" Remo said.

The chief nodded. "They are his weapons. The birds keep us here. When he needs to kill, he sends the birds. They return bloated, with the blood of my village in them."

Remo remembered the giant gulls squatting on the island's shore. "And the airstrip—that's his too?"

The chief looked at him, confused. "The road," Remo explained. "The road leading to the ocean."

"Zoran gets all he wishes. One day his men came from the sea with sacks and machines. Soon the road was built. But no one used the road. His men ordered us to cover it up. Then one day we were ordered to uncover it. As soon as we were finished, a strange airplane as fast as lightning came upon it, and we covered the road again."

"What happened to the plane?"

Timu gazed down into the valley, where already a swarm of uniformed men was emerging from the mouth of the rock cluster and making their way upward through the brush toward the cliff tops. "It is Zoran's, gone forever to his cave with the white man who flew it." Timu looked around nervously. "Now you must go. Zoran's men are coming. We will distract them."

"What happens to you if we escape?" Chiun asked.

"Do not be concerned, Master," Timu said.

"You know damned well what'll happen, Little Father," Remo said. "But it doesn't matter. We're not going anywhere anyway."

"No," Timu said. "I forbid you to stay. He will kill you."

"If Chiun and I both leave, he'll kill you." The soldiers were moving quickly up the hills. It would be a matter of seconds before they spotted the tribe and its two visitors. Remo clasped Chiun's arm.

"Listen," he said. "That plane's here, and I've got to find out what's going on. But Smitty's got to know now. Take the boat back to the mainland and tell him we found the plane."

"Call him yourself," Chiun said. "I do not use telephones. Why do I not stay and you go?"

"Because, dammit, you're all involved with this tribe and some legend or something, and the plane's the only thing that's important right now. That's our contract, Chiun. It's what we've got to do."

Chiun thought for a moment. "I was growing tired of this island anyway," he said. "It is impossible to sleep here with all this noise."

"Good," said Remo.

"And you must let no harm come to these people. They are under my protection," Chiun said.

"You've got it," Remo said.

In an instant, Chiun was gone, without a sound, vanished into the forest, leaving not so much as a twisted twig to mark his path.

When the soldiers arrived, Remo was ready.

To be captured.

To find out who Zoran was and where the stolen plane was.

Chapter Seven

The stone wall of a tidy little house surrounded by geraniums blew into fragments. The ceiling, collapsing with the crash of roof beams, emitted a puff of white dust as if it were the cottage's dying sigh. From the wreckage stepped a tall blonde woman, despairing yet proud, clutching the lifeless body of her infant.

Caan snickered. The good part was coming next. He blinked and rubbed his red-rimmed eyes as the familiar "enemy" faces, grotesque caricatures of leering, big-nosed American soldiers, filled the white wall opposite his bed.

"The destruction of a perfect world," he chanted along with the ostensibly grief-stricken announcer.

The film snapped and the image disappeared, leaving only a blank wall and the flapping of the broken film in the projector. The noise didn't matter. Caan had not heard silence since arriving in this place—this room, this bed. And the other, the room it was best not to think about. Just a few days it had been, and already his universe had shrunk to two rooms.

He rubbed the bristly stubble on his chin. It was more than shadow; this was the beginning of a beard, he thought idly, smacking his tongue against the roof of his mouth. He was so thirsty. God, and so tired.

Was there to be no rest for him at all? Was it the Angel's price for passing him over with its wings of death?

Birds. Lepers. Crazy talk.

He shook his head violently to clear it. He stared at the blank wall. Caan hadn't realized till that moment that the film wasn't running. How many times had he seen it? A hundred? A thousand? The decimation of Aryan Germany at the hands of the world's archfiend, America, had flashed before him in this room so often that at times he was sure he was losing his mind.

"Lieutenant Junior Grade Richard A. Caan, U.S. Navy, 124258486," he said in a loud voice, sitting up as straight as he could with the metal straps holding his ankles to the bed. Name, rank, and serial number. That was all he was obliged to give.

But God, if he could just sleep! Maybe if he sneaked up on it, curled himself into a position where it didn't seem as though he was lying down . . . It didn't work. As soon as his back touched the mattress, an electric shock coursed through Caan's body like an eel.

He sat up. An involuntary sob caught in his

63

throat. *Don't*, he warned himself. *Don't let them break you.*

"Lieutenant Junior Grade Richard A. Caan, U.S. Navy, 124258486," he said again, his voice quavering as the film in the projector flapped noisily nearby.

"We know who you are," a voice at the door said pleasantly in softly accented English. Caan looked up, even though he knew with certain dread who it was.

The door closed with a soft click. The lights came on, stabbing Caan's worn-out eyes. The white man limped past Caan to the projector and shut it off.

The White Man. That was what Caan had privately named the old lunatic, since white was his most distinguishing external characteristic. He was old, nearly seventy, from the looks of him, with snow-white hair, powder-white skin, and a white laboratory coat sheathing his round belly. He wore glasses trimmed with thin gold rims. Behind them stared a pair of eyes as blue as sky and as cold as ice.

"Where's my plane?" Caan demanded, trying to sit up straight. His posture would, he thought, lend more authority to his words.

"It's nearby," the White Man said. "You'll see it before long."

The door opened again, and two young soldiers entered and walked briskly to Caan's bedside. As usual, one held Caan's arms locked behind him while the other unfastened the ankle straps.

He didn't resist. The routine was too familiar

by now. The bed, the endless, bloody movies on the wall, the white man, the soldiers. And The Room.

"Don't take me," Caan said in a small voice shaking with fear. "Please."

The White Man smiled briefly, a crisp acknowledgement of his own successful efforts. Then he gestured to the two soldiers.

"Not the room," Caan howled, the sound utterly out of control, half-moan, half-scream, with a hint of question in it. "I can't go there. . . ."

The soldiers dragged him from the bed.

To The Room.

In The Room, which was an operating room, a white bird flapped from its perch to light on the White Man's shoulder as Caan was being strapped onto one of the two flat metal tables there. The White Man stroked the gull, cooing lovingly, then turned to inspect the tray of arcane surgical instruments that had been wheeled to Caan's side.

"Thank you," he said to the two soldiers. He removed the bird from his shoulder and handed it to one of the men. With a nod, they left.

Caan's breathing quickened as the other man snapped on a pair of rubber gloves with easy expertise.

"You do not have to be here," he said. "Just agree to perform the mission, and you'll never see this room again."

Caan blinked silently. The White Man's icy eyes moved closer, peering at him from above the gold-rimmed spectacles. "You will have exercise and good food and companionship. Perhaps even a room with flowers where you can sleep. Wouldn't you like to sleep, Mr. Caan?" he teased.

"But . . . " Caan caught himself blubbering, and stopped.

The White Man bent over solicitously. "But what? Go ahead, speak. It will help us both to talk together, don't you think?"

"The mission," Caan said.

The White Man smiled, again only with his lips. The cold eyes still bored into Caan's. "That's all," he said with studied patience. "Just one flight. Before the flight, you'll be treated with care and respect. Afterward, you will be free. You will never have to return here."

"But you're asking me to destroy my country!" Caan screamed. "My *country*."

The smile clicked off like a mechanism. "You are a Jew," the White Man said with loathing. "You have no country."

There was no more talk. He picked up one of the metal instruments, held it up to the light, and pressed it behind Caan's ear. As the metal touched flesh, a single image crossed Caan's terrified mind. A strange image, incongruous under the circumstances: it was a memory of his grandmother sitting in the stuffed brown rocking chair in her living room, a crocheted antimacassar behind her head.

The pilot's first scream echoed through the cave. As he weakened, they grew faint.

Chapter Eight

Remo waited in an isolated chamber of the cave complex. Two orange vinyl settees were the only furniture. The rest of the room was bare except for the shelves lining all four stone walls, fitted with Latin-labeled specimen jars containing various sorts of tissue. A solitary finger, half eaten by disease, floated in one. Others held organs, human embryos, and skin samples. Some full limbs floated in covered plastic vats, neatly labeled and piled in a corner. They bore little resemblance to human beings, but one thing was certain: all the bodily parts lining the shelves had once belonged to lepers.

He almost dropped a jar filled with lung tissue when he heard the pilot's scream. It came from somewhere nearby, but the deceptive echoes of the cave dispersed the sound so that it seemed to come from everywhere. Remo replaced the jar and moved over to the window, which had been chiseled out of solid rock.

No guards surrounded the opening, and only four iron bars separated the room from the rest of the valley. Beyond, the leper village stood like a Nativity tableau. A row of fat white birds perched on the sill outside, placed and watchful.

With a click the door opened and Ana stepped inside. Her eyes were glassy and dreamy. They passed over Remo as if he weren't there.

"What happened to you?" he asked.

The girl sat primly on one of the settees, straight-backed and silent. She stared straight ahead.

"Ana, you've got to talk to me. What's going on? Why'd you run away from me like that?"

Her smile reminded Remo of the Mona Lisa's, demure and faintly questioning.

"Don't you even remember me?"

She shook her head slowly, her eyes never quite meeting his.

"Who's Zoran?" he asked.

Her brow furrowed.

"Who's Zoran?"

She clapped her hands over her ears.

"Who's Zoran?" he repeated.

"Stop!" she shrieked.

The door opened quietly. Caan's "white man," the bird again perched on his shoulder, entered. He was brisk and efficient, paying attention only to the girl. With a yank, he pulled her head back so that her terrified eyes were on him. He passed a hand near her face several times in a quick wave. She grew quiet, her expression soft and lost.

After a moment, he stepped back and looked

Remo up and down in cool appraisal. "I am Zoran," he said. "Although knowledge of my identity will not be of much use to you."

"What have you done to her?" Remo demanded.

Zoran chuckled. "You Americans have always fancied yourselves heroes." He walked to the far end of the room, picked up a specimen jar, and fondled it distractedly. Ana here has told me that you are much respected among her people." He continued to look at Remo for a moment after he spoke, then burst suddenly into a bout of loud, coarse laughter. "Her people. Lepers. The dregs of the human race. Nature's irreparable mistakes, the discards of evolution. How does it feel to be king of the lepers?"

Ana continued to sit silently, oblivious to what was being said.

"You the guy who did this?" Remo asked, sweeping his arm to indicate a row of pickled fetuses.

"Oh, they do have their uses, I suppose," Zoran said with chilling whimsy. "The lepers, I mean."

"I can guess what use you have for them."

Zoran snapped to attention. "My experiments are for the good of mankind," he said hotly. "They always have been. By using as test cases an inferior group of humans—humans for whom the rest of humanity has no use—a scientist can further the world's knowledge of the human organism and its possibilities by great bounds rather than by the slow inches of animal research and laboratory mathematics. Do you

70

understand me?" He dismissed Remo with a flick of his wrist. "No, of course not."

"Don't give yourself so much credit," Remo said. "You're not the first creep to try your so-called 'experiments' on human beings. The concentration camps in World War Two were full of your kind."

"*Their* kind, you mean," Zoran corrected, pointing to the specimen jars with a smile. "There are always more laboratory rats than there are laboratory researchers."

The sight of the man disgusted Remo. He turned to the window, where the birds crowded one another with shoves and angry squawks. One of them pecked viciously at the bird next to it. It drew blood. The recipient of the blow fluttered upward for a moment, spraying dots of red over its glossy wing feathers, then swooped onto its attacker's chest with talons like razors. With its victim screeching and jerking beneath it, the bird thrust its beak into the soft white neck and, in an instant of gory triumph, tore out its throat, still throbbing with its heartbeat. The dead bird's head rolled back, bathed in its own blood.

Suddenly it all made sense. "These birds killed the crew of the *Andrew Jackson*," Remo said flatly, knowing it to be true.

"Very perceptive." He stroked the feathers of the gull on his shoulder. "Actually, it was the simplest sort of genetic engineering. But you see, the lepers made it all possible," he said expansively. "Another giant leap for mankind." The half-moon smile on his lips broadened.

"You make me sick," Remo said.

Zoran shrugged. "All great men are misunderstood."

"What'd you do with the pilot?"

"Caan? He is resting in his bed, catching up on his American history, I believe. Rather a crash course."

At least Caan was still alive, if Zoran was telling the truth. "And the plane?"

"Somewhere, somewhere." He waved his arms as if the capture of the F-24 were a subject too trivial for discussion. He strode over to Ana. "Now this," he said, touching the girl's face with his stubby fingers. "This is my finest case. Raise your arm, Ana."

Silently, without changing her vacant expression, the girl obeyed. "She's always most susceptible after one of her attacks."

"Attacks? You mean the screaming fit she went into in the mountains?"

"Shhh." His eyes focused on the girl's, Zoran plucked a long needle from inside one of the pockets of his lab coat and pushed it roughly through the girl's arm.

"What the *hell* . . ."

It came cleanly out the other side. Zoran removed it, and the girl brought it back to rest on her lap, uncaring about the thin streams of blood oozing from the wounds.

"Anything is possible," Zoran said in a tone close to ecstasy. "With enough time, I can do anything."

There was a brief, sharp knock at the door. It opened crisply, and a soldier walked to Zoran, whispering something in his ear. He listened, laughed, and looked with interest out the window.

He handed the bird on his shoulder to the soldier. "Get it outside within ten seconds," he said. He waved at Ana. "Take the girl, too. I've had enough of her for the moment."

The guard rushed out, clutching the bird in one hand like a time bomb, and the girl in the other. "Ten," Zoran said, looking intently at his wristwatch. He counted off the seconds. "Four, three, two, one." He pressed a button on the side of the watch.

Outside, the birds whipped into a frenzy. Remo's hearing, long trained to detect sounds the ordinary human ear couldn't perceive, picked up a shattering ultrasonic frequency.

"What's that for?" he asked, wincing.

Zoran gazed at him with new appreciation. "I'm surprised you could even hear it. You must be quiet a remarkable specimen yourself," he said. "The sound is meant for the birds."

From the window Remo could see them flying, squawking wildly, in all directions.

"It has long been known that certain aquatic mammals, particularly the common dolphin, respond to a certain sound frequency by exhibiting unusually active and aggressive behavior. I simply applied the same principle to my genetically enlarged gulls, testing them at each quarter-tone past human range before I found exactly the right note. *Voilà*. My secrets are exposed." He cocked his head in a courtly gesture.

"Is that how you got them to attack the ship?"

"Of course."

"How did you direct them to it?"

He gave Remo a let's-not-be-silly grin. "They follow the direction of the signal," he said.

"Where's the signal going now?" Remo asked.

Zoran's countenance brightened. "Why, of course, to your friend, the old Oriental. My men saw him on shore, trying to escape."

"Good luck," Remo said. "Your birds have as much chance against him as raindrops do." But from the village, he heard the screams of those who had gotten in the birds' path as they sped toward the shoreline. And Chiun.

"Do not be too sure. Some men aboard the ship, the *Andrew Jackson*, tried to escape by going overboard and underwater," Zoran said. "The birds will wait. Eventually everyone must come up to the surface. When they do, the birds pluck out their eyes. The rest is easy. The old man is as good as dead."

Remo hesitated. Even Chiun had to come up for air. Suppose Zoran were right and the birds were still waiting. Could even Chiun? . . . .

"I think it's about time somebody canceled your reservation," Remo said coldly.

"It is too late for the old man. Only I can call the birds off."

"Then do it," Remo said.

Zoran shook his head. "I have waited all these years for my moment. Do you think even pain could deflect me now from my course?

74

Nothing can. Only you can save the old man's life," he said.

"How? Remo said.

Zoran clapped his hands, and two uniformed soldiers entered the room.

"You will go with my men," he said.

Remo nodded. "Call off the birds," he said.

Zoran held up his wristwatch. He placed his index finger against the button on the side. He nodded to his two guards, and they came up and took Remo's arm and pulled him toward the door of the room.

Remo's back was to Zoran when suddenly he felt the sharp ping of a needle entering his lower back. Almost instantly, his fine-tuned system felt a drug coursing through his veins. He staggered slightly, but the guards held him up.

As he was passing into unconsciousness, he heard Zoran cackle behind him.

"Fool," the old man hissed. "There is no calling off my birds. The old Oriental is dead."

Chapter Nine

Swift flows the day
As the waters of life
Recede toward the Void.

Thus chanted Chiun, 102nd Master of the Glorious House of Sinanju, as he entered the small boat. He looked up toward the purple-streaked sky of dawn. It was a perfect morning. Dew glistened on the lush jungle leaves of the island. Sand sparkled in the rising sun. The fragrant air was filled with bird songs. And he had just composed a verse of Ung poetry befitting the Great First Master Wang himself.

"Swift flows the day," he repeated, settling his robes around him. "As . . ." He frowned. "Swift flows the day as . . ."

As what? He rowed a few yards. "As the day flows?" he asked aloud. His almond eyes narrowed. "Swift flows the day as . . ."

Enraged, he jumped up and down in the boat, causing it to rock precariously. To forget the finest example of Ung poetry since Wang! To deny the prosaic world his flight of genius!

"Swift flows the day," he bellowed, making it sound like a mortal threat. He was so preoccupied with his poem that the first attacking bird

77

almost hit its target. Shrieking, its wide wings brushed past Chiun's whirling body as the old man ducked, sending the bird crashing head-first into the sea.

Seconds behind the lead bird flew a wedge of huge gulls, awesome in their battle formation. Following the electronic signal, they swooped downward toward Chiun like fighter planes.

Water. Something about water, Chiun thought distractedly as the birds fairly whistled in their descent. "Swift flows the water . . ."

When the birds were inches away from him, he dived. From beneath the clear water, he saw the boat torn to fragments on the churning surface as the crazed gulls went about their work. He slowed his heartbeat and propelled himself deeper and farther out to sea.

This was a world he had loved ever since he had first discovered its secrets nearly eighty years ago off the frozen, rocky shores of Sinanju. It was a place of peace and violent beauty, where tubeworms grew in clusters as big as gladioli, and moonlight-colored crabs scuttled for shelter as the great hunter fish searched out their first prey of the day.

He lowered his temperature to keep from getting cold in the icy depths. As a child of ten, he had remained underwater for seven hours, watching, listening, fascinated. The journey to Key West was much shorter, less than an hour. Still, he smiled as he raced through the underwater kingdom, an unobtrusive visitor passing through.

78

He had spent so much time with Remo over the past ten years that he had all but forgotten the simple pleasures of his youth. With his extraordinarily delicate hands, he brushed the petals of a sea dandelion and tickled the pale underbelly of a young blue whale. At his touch, the whale wiggled slightly, enjoying the sensation.

He would show this to Remo, he decided. Someday, when the boy was ready, when his anger and disappointment and impatience were spent, when Remo's scars from his earlier life had healed.

Rocks loomed ahead, signaling the far end of Florida's massive living reef, thick with underwater life. Halfway across the reef, a group of divers paddled cumbersomely, their metal tanks bobbing on their backs. One of them pointed at Chiun, a burst of bubbles rising from his open mouth. Another diver fluttered upward, his flippers wriggling frantically. Two more tried to swim to meet the ancient Korean clad in his silk brocade kimono, but they were too slow. Chiun was speeding toward shore faster than a barracuda.

When he emerged near Port Zachary Taylor, he looked back and saw a vast flight of birds heading back toward the lepers' island. It was unimportant. He had remembered the rest of the poem.

On land he found a telephone booth, lifted the receiver to his ear, waited for the operator. "Swift flows the day," he began, trying not to forget the verse again. Nothing happened.

"This is the Master of Sinanju," he yelled irritably into the mouthpiece. "Perform your duty, or be smitten into nothingness."

A passerby, an elegant woman of middle years, peered in discreetly. "Halt," Chiun commanded. The woman blushed, and her hand fluttered to her chest. Chiun stepped out and bowed politely. "Most gracious lady, I wish to know the location of another telephone machine. This one does not work, exactly like everything else in this lunatic country."

'Why, you have to put in a dime first," the lady drawled in soft Southern tones as she backed away from him.

"A dime?"

"Ten cents. Do you have a dime?"

"I will not pay tribute to speak to a servant," he said stubbornly.

"Tribute?"

"Tribute. Riches earned by assassinating the enemies of your government."

The woman blanched. "Wh—what?"

Chiun beamed. "I am an assassin, madam. Chiun, Master of Sinanju. Perhaps you've heard of me."

"Go ahead, take my money," she shrilled, thrusting her pocketbook at Chiun.

He pushed it back toward her with a deprecating gesture. "Thank you, kind lady, but I have no use for a woman's handbag. I wish only to learn the whereabouts of a telephone machine which does not require tribute."

"But they all take a dime," she said.

Chiun reddened. "Foul machines." He rushed

back inside the booth, lifted the receiver, and shouted, "Hear me, O lowly servant's tool. Be warned your demand for tribute will not be met. Prepare to meet your doom."

He delivered a rocking blow to the machine with the heel of his hand. It came so fast that the air inside the booth compressed and shattered the glass of the booth. A two-finger punch sent the glass tinkling to the earth in fragments. The woman outside fainted. A third thrust, and the telephone sprang away from the wall as a stream of dimes poured from the coin return like a Los Vegas slot machine paying off.

Chiun held his cupped hands beneath the falling money. When they were full, he brought the coins to the woman, who was just coming to on the sidewalk, plucked one dime from the top, and poured the rest into her lap. "Tribute," he said debonairly. "For your assistance and gracious beauty." He bowed again.

As she poured the dimes into her purse and staggered away, still dazed, Chiun made his way back to the splintered telephone. He inserted his dime, pressed the operator's button and demanded to be connected with Emperor Smith at Folcroft Sanitarium in Rye, New York.

Eventually, the lemony voice answered, "Yes?"

"Swift flows the day as the waters of life recede toward the Void," Chiun said in his best oratory style.

After some time, the voice on the other end said, "I see."

"It is Ung poetry. The finest since Wang."

81

"Hmmm," Smith said. "Chiun, is it you?"

Chiun's lips tightened in annoyance. "Of course I am I, Emperor," he said. "Who else would I be? Who else would call to sing your praises?"

"Well, uh . . . may I ask why you're calling on this line? Is Remo all right?"

"Remo is Remo," Chiun said indifferently. "He has remained with the lepers."

"The what?"

"He is on an island of great white birds which attack like locusts. With a road that sends those upon it into the depths of the sea."

Smith tallied this information. "Could you explain that more clearly, please?"

"What is to explain?" Chiun answered, already beginning to feel the annoyance that always accompanied conversation with Smith. He sighed. "Remo and I found the place where your airplane may be. An island. It is inhabited by lepers from the island of Molokai."

There was a sharp intake of breath on the other end. "Molokai?" Smith asked softly. "Are you sure?"

Chiun sputtered. "Of course I am sure. It is one of the chain of Hawaiian islands."

"Did you see the plane there?"

"How can one see underground?" Chiun answered grouchily. "But there is a cave, guarded by soldiers and birds."

"What kind of soldiers?"

"Who knows? White men. They all look the same."

"I see. Anything else?"

"No. There was a minor incident, but surely it does not warrant your valuable time, mighty Emperor Smith."

"I'd like to hear it anyway."

"It is of no consequence. It concerns Remo."

"I'd like to hear it," Smith repeated patiently.

Chiun sighed. "Very well. As usual, my ungrateful pupil, in pursuit of a woman, incurred the wrath of the leader of the soldiers, and has been momentarily detained on the island."

"Oh. Is that serious? Can he escape?"

"Of course he can escape. He is my pupil. He has remained of his own will, in order to speak with someone called Zoran."

This time the silence was of some duration. "Zoran?" Smith asked finally, his voice breathless. In the background, the Folcroft computers began to bleep and chatter. "Zoran?"

"Yes, *Zoran*," Chiun said, shifting the phone from one ear to the other. "Emperor, if you wish no other service, I will continue the insignificant things which make up an old man's life. . . ."

"*Don't move*," Smith commanded in a tone Chiun had never heard before. "Where are you?"

"I am speaking from a telephone in Florida," Chiun answered archly.

"Where? Key West?"

"I believe that is the place."

"Go to the naval base there and wait for me. Chiun, are you listening?"

"Yes," he said, yawning.

"This is very important. More important than I can tell you. Please do as I say."

"Your wish is my command, Emperor," Chiun said enthusiastically. "Naturally, for my extra effort, I assume my humble village of Sinanju will receive further tribute beyond our agreed fee."

"We'll see. Wait for me."

"One moment, Emperor. You see, I am an old man. I fear my powers of recall are not what they once were in the flowering of my youth. This island, it is so far and difficult to find—"

"Okay," Smith said. "Additional tribute."

"South by southwest, latitude eighty-two degrees by twenty-four degrees longitude."

"Wait for me," Smith said. "And once and for all, I am not an emperor."

"You are too modest, O generous and illustrious one," Chiun said.

He left the receiver dangling from its cord and walked out into the street, wondering. The crazy Emperor Smith was becoming crazier every day. Was he actually seeking to go along on Remo's mission? A middle-aged white man with a business suit and a briefcase?

He shrugged once and dismissed it from his thoughts. If Smith felt like getting killed on a jungle island, that was his business. As long as the extra tribute was paid in advance.

Chapter Ten

LUSTBADEN, ZORAN

B. 1912, BERLIN, GERMANY
B.S. UNIV. HEIDELBERG, 1928
M.D. HEIDELBERG, 1932,
SUMMA CUM LAUDE
OCC: PHYSICIAN (GENETICS)
UNMARRIED

BACKGROUND: PRECOCIOUS GENETICIST RE-
CRUITED PERSONALLY BY ADOLF HITLER IN
1938 TO SERVE UNDER JOSEF MENGELE AS
ASSISTANT FOR GENETIC EXPERIMENTS WITH
CONCENTRATION CAMP INMATES AT AUSCH-
WITZ, PRESENTLY WANTED BY WAR CRIMES
COMMISSION FOR DIRECT PARTICIPATION IN
TORTURE AND DEATH OF 40,000 PERSONS AS
RESULT OF EXPERIMENTS WITH PITUITARY
MALFUNCTIONS. SUBJECT IS ADEPT WITH
TECHNIQUES OF HYPNOSIS. UNVERIFIED
SIGHTING OF SUBJECT 11/21/55, BUENOS
AIRES, ARGENTINA. UNVERIFIED SIGHTING
OF SUBJECT 6/1/62, MOLOKAI, HAWAII. *EX-
TREMELY DANGEROUS*. DETAILS IN CIA RE-
PORT #36121055.

The supersonic test plane that had taken Smith on as a passenger by direct order of the President of the United States screamed at 60,000 feet toward the Key West Naval Station.

He folded the printout. He didn't need to see file #36121055. He had written it.

Molokai, 1962. It was one of his last assignments for the CIA, and he had failed then, as he had failed in Buenos Aires in '55. Lustbaden had eluded him all his professional career.

But Zoran Lustbaden had had help. SPIDER, the network of Nazi officers organized just before the end of the war to aid their members in escaping justice for their crimes, had everything: money siphoned from the Third Reich's remaining funds after Hitler's death, escape routes through Europe and South America and the little-known, practically unexplorable islands of the Pacific, and bodies—young, secret recruits from all over the western world who had been brainwashed into believing Hitler's ideal of Aryan supremacy. These young men willingly left their homes, jobs, and families to serve SPIDER's exiled leaders as bodyguards, drivers, servants, consultants, and, when necesary, soldiers.

SPIDER's chain was unbreakable. For thirty-six years it had protected Josef Mengele himself, the white-gloved "Angel of Death" whose experiments with children at Auschwitz had caused the world to wail in horror and grief. And Mengele's face was well known, photographed often and reprinted in publications from Berlin to Shanghai.

Zoran Lustbaden, Mengele's assistant, was less visible. Or perhaps just smarter. Conspicuous in the Nazi ranks for his modesty among a group of officers famous the world over for their arrogance, Lustbaden always declined to be photographed, even on state occasions. Likewise, his name was rarely mentioned in Mengele's numerous reports to Hitler and Goebbels. He had no wife and no children to write to, no one Smith could use as leverage against him. Lustbaden was the perfect SPIDER protégé: No ties, no records, no one to remember him.

No one but the few concentration camp survivors who still carried scars from the wounds Zoran Lustbaden had inflicted.

Smith opened his briefcase, placed the computer printout inside, and extracted a yellowed print of a photograph taken nearly fifty years before. It was a blowup of one face in a group portrait of the 1932 graduating class of the Heidelberg University Medical School.

The face was that of a boy. The young genius Lustbaden had been only twenty when it was taken. He had stood, with typical self-effacement, at the far edge of the group, his face darkened by shadows and turned slightly inward toward the rest of the class, so that he was in three-quarter profile.

Still, it was a face Smith had stamped indelibly into his brain: the pale, cold eyes, eerily translucent in the grainy black and white photograph, the stooping shoulders, the stocky body already going to fat, the sly half-curve of the mouth. A man who smiled without his eyes.

The Prince of Hell.

That was how Lustbaden was known at Auschwitz, where his victims, convulsing from his injections into the glands in their throats, watched the cold eyes and the half-moon smile as they listened, in the spaces between their own screams, to his soothing lies.

Smith closed his eyes. They burned from fatigue. Except for a few scattered moments on the sofa in his office, he had not slept in two days. CURE was becoming so big, so complex. The small secret organization that had been formed to deter crime had become a massive responsibility. Even with a human weapon like Remo at his disposal, Smith needed the skill of a magician, the patience of a monk, and a brain as tireless as the computers at Folcroft to get through each day. There was simply too much crime, and Smith was feeling his age. Tasks that had once seemed effortless were becoming monumentally difficult, and his reflexes were slowing.

He had possessed enviable reflexes once. Not like Remo's, of course, but as good as those of any man in the OSS, which had its share of good men. In the blurry red images of near-sleep, Smith saw himself running, running through the gutted, Nazi-infested streets of Warsaw in January of 1943, with the twang of bullets at his back and the acrid smell of spent gunfire all around him. His cover had been blown sky high in the middle of a delicate maneuver with a group of Polish Resistance fighters.

One of them had been working for the Nazis all along. By the time Smith found out about it, every member of the tough little group had been killed, and the SS was closing in on him fast.

It had been pure chance that had brought him to the dead-end alley strewn with the clotheslines and garbage of the poor. A wall stood—inexplicably, he remembered thinking—at the far end of the alley. The gunshots at its open end were too close for escape. There was nowhere to go.

Above him, a wiry, small man in black trousers and a ragged overcoat, with a face like so many Poles in those days—thin, creased, bearing a permanent expression of crushing anxiety—sat smoking on the fire escape of a crumbling brick building. Without a word, Smith had held his hand up to him. The man saw the gesture, stood up, and walked into the building.

It was Smith's last, desperate card, and he had drawn a joker. There was nothing left to do but wait for the Luger that would fire the first shot at him. And hope that first shot killed him.

Then, out of the sky, a rope fell within inches of him. The man on the fire escape, his hand-rolled cigarette dangling from his mouth, was tying his end around his waist. When he was done, he clasped the rope with his powerful, slender hands and nodded to Smith.

The man moved with the calm swiftness of one who'd grown accustomed to the necessities of war. He helped Smith over the landing and pushed him into the building while he yanked up the rope with ease.

Inside the shabby apartment, a woman and three children, a teenage girl and twin boys around six years of age, accepted him without question, even though he was not in uniform and had not spoken a word. The woman wrapped a blanket around him. Till then, Smith hadn't even realized he was cold.

Once safe in the shadows of the dark apartment, however, he allowed himself to shiver. The woman adjusted the threadbare blanket around him more tightly and gave him a motherly smile at the end of her ministrations. Like her husband, she was thin, but Smith could see from the excess skin around her face and neck that thinness was not her proper state. In better times she would have been one of those women who complain good-naturedly about needing to go on a diet while serving platters heaped with piroghi and halupki.

The girl, a breathtaking beauty even at her young age, with blonde hair and enormous seagreen eyes, brought him soup. Smith refused it, guessing it was all they had, but the mother insisted. He drank it gratefully and, afterward, slept.

He awoke in a cold sweat, uncertain for the moment where he was, confused by the darkness of the tiny apartment. He must have cried out in his sleep because, as soon as his panic subsided, he noticed the man's arm on his.

"Whoever you are, you are safe," the man said in Polish.

"Why did you help me?" Smith asked.

"Because the Nazis were after you."

"Is that why you used a rope?"

The man nodded. "I do not trust the neighbors on the ground floor."

"Do you belong to the Resistance?" Smith asked.

The man looked Smith squarely in the eye. "We are Jews," he said.

Smith stayed with them—their family name was Jevsevar—for five days. During the day, Dimi, the man who had saved his life, and Smith, disguised in Dimi's rags and passed off to family acquaintances as a visiting cousin, went foraging for food among the few shops still operating in the city.

Dimi expressed his admiration for Smith's abilities as a thief. Smith himself was not particularly proud of stealing, for whatever reason, and in later years would never mention the episode to anyone, not even his wife.

At night, the Jevsevars amused themselves with stories while Smith pored over maps, seeking an escape route out of Poland for himself and the Jevsevars.

On the sixth day the Nazis came.

Their unmistakable footsteps pounded up the rickety stariway. The beating at the door began. Dimi shoved Smith out the fire escape and up onto the roof.

"Run," he said. "Over the rooftops, toward the river. Most of the buildings are abandoned there."

"Get your family. We'll all go."

Dimi shook his head. "My boys are too young, and Helena is not strong. My place is with them. Hurry."

Smith watched the wiry man with the strong hands walk back to the fire escape. "Thank you," he said. He never knew afterward if Dimi had heard him or not.

The Jevsevars were taken to Auschwitz. From his post as an OSS strategist in London over two years later, Smith was able to book passage on an army convoy headed for Poland amid the Allied victory celebrations. After weeks of false leads, he finally tracked down Dimi Jevsevar in a seamy rooming house outside the town of Piekielko.

He was still wiry, but his calm strength had been replaced by a haunted emptiness. His hands trembled, and he had difficulty remembering. He knew Smith, but had forgotten the circumstances, mistaking him for a distant relative. His hair had turned white.

Dimi's family was gone. The twin boys were the first to die, courtesy of Mengele's and Lustbaden's experiments with chromosomal alteration. His wife, Helena, neither healthy nor particularly beautiful, outlived her usefulness shortly afterward. She was claimed by the gas chambers. The girl with the sea-green eyes, Dimi's daughter, was used as Zoran's private prostitute until she took her own life with a jagged piece of a discarded liquor bottle across her wrists.

There was nothing left. A trace in Buenos Aires . . . too late. SPIDER had reached Lustbaden before Smith. A whisper near the leper colony at Molokai seven years later. . . . He was gone, fled with a group of patients from the colony and his SPIDER corps.

And then, for twenty years, nothing. The Prince of Hell had vanished.

Smith awoke with a start, surprised to hear the roar of jet engines. His fingers had plastered themselves to the photograph on his lap, and when he removed them, they left prints over Lustbaden's half-moon smile.

I have known you for too long, Smith thought, looking at the picture and seeing only the face of pure evil.

The search would end soon. One of them was going to die.

He opened his briefcase, arranged its contents, and set the photograph carefully inside.

Chapter Eleven

And so it came to pass that the elderly Chiun, regarded by his employer as a bizarre, if competent, adjunct to the enforcer arm of CURE, and Harold W. Smith, notable among his employees as the most boring man in the world, set out together for the Valley of the Damned.

Smith had commandeered a Navy speedboat, and was at the helm. As usual, the two men had little to say to each other, since both despised small talk. Smith steered the vessel toward the island, following Chiun's terse directions. Chiun reveled silently in the exhilarating wind that shot into their faces in the open boat.

Locking his briefcase in a watertight compartment, Smith moored the craft at a deserted, rocky spot some distance from the concealed path. Careful not to disturb the birds gathered there, they made their way through the jungle brush to the airstrip.

"We think it is here that Zoran brought your missing airplane," Chiun said.

"I see," Smith answered noncommitally.

Chiun yawned and moved on. Nothing interested Smith. Nothing. Chiun vowed he would write an Ung poem about Smith one day, if he could keep from falling asleep while composing it.

The residents of the valley were holding some sort of ceremony. As far distant as the shore, Smith and Chiun could hear the tribal chant of the whole village.

Timu, garbed in ceremonial robes and a high feather headdress, looked at the two men in surprise when they approached.

"Master," he said, bowing low to Chiun. "You live. We were certain the birds had killed you—with these others." He gestured toward a stack of long objects the size of human beings, swathed in black cloth.

"These are your dead?" Smith asked.

The chief eyed him suspiciously.

"He is the Emperor of my son's tribe," Chiun whispered to the chief. "He brings no harm."

Solemnly Timu bowed to Smith. He raised a carved wooden staff. The villagers, chanting in front of their huts, moved slowly toward the pile and picked up the black-draped bundles.

"These represent our dead," Timu explained. "They are only sticks wrapped in cloth. We are not permitted to keep the bodies of our murdered people." His mouth curved down bitterly. "Zoran needs the corpses for his own purposes."

The villagers formed a double-circle, chanting as they carried the effigies high over their heads.

"How were they murdered?" Smith asked.

"The birds," Timu said wearily. "Again," He turned to Chiun. "We thought you were among our losses today. Portions of your boat were found, smashed to pieces."

Timu shouted something in an ancient Hawaiian dialect, and an old man stepped out of the double-circle of mourners. He was carrying a black-shrouded effigy set apart from the others by a gold stripe. "This was your effigy, O Master of Sinanju. I am pleased to remove it from our funeral." He unwrapped the black cloth slowly and scattered the sticks on the ground. "You were brave and kind to return to us."

"We wish to help you," Chiun said. "Only you must no longer be afraid to tell us the truth."

Timu looked at the villagers, helplessly grieving over their families and neighbors. In the distance, beneath the high-domed rocks, the bodies of those dead were awaiting Zoran's mutilation. The Master of Sinanju's own son was somewhere in that cave, possibly already under Zoran's knife with the others.

"I will tell you all I know," Timu said.

The funeral ended, the chief led them to his hut. At the doorway, he said, "We can speak here—outside—if you wish."

"I am not frightened of your ailment," Smith said.

They went inside. Timu gave Chiun the place of honor, facing the narrow doorway, with Smith to his right. He began slowly, as if he had rehearsed the telling of his story many times over the years.

"He was always called Zoran, nothing more. He is a doctor, although he does not wish to be addressed that way."

Smith felt his heart quicken. "A German?" he asked. It was the same man. It had to be.

"A foreigner," the chief said. "He came to Molokai, where my people lived, many years ago. He did not practice at the main hospital, but in his own clinic, where he accepted only the worst cases—those the hospital could no longer treat. He made miraculous cures. Dying men who could hardly breathe walked with ease under his care. Women whose bodies had been damaged beyond repair by sickness were able to bear children. We looked on him as a god."

Smith nodded. There was no doubt that Zoran Lustbaden had a brilliant medical mind. Josef Mengele himself had said as much in one of his rare references to his associate.

"While my sister Ana went to college, she worked in Zoran's clinic. She continued after she began medical school. He was her hero in those days," the chief said ruefully. "It was her dream to become like him, to take over his clinic after he died. Then—the thing—happened. The terrible event." Timu squeezed his eyes shut as he struggled with his emotions.

Chiun laid a delicate hand on the chief's arm. "Try to tell us everything," he said. "It will help."

"Please," Smith urged.

Timu swallowed. "Yes. It is necessary," he said grimly. He steeled himself with a deep breath. "One day while she was walking to the clinic, she was violated by a group of men. She was raped and beaten almost to death. Zoran himself found her and took her to his clinic. It was weeks before she regained consciousness. Since she was covered with cuts, he isolated her from us until she was completely healed, to protect her from the contamination of leprosy. We did not see her for six months."

"Who did this to her?" Smith asked.

"She did not remember. She still does not remember. Not a face, nothing. Only that there were many men."

He shook his head. "After that, she was changed. She never left the colony again, and could no longer work at the clinic. She chose to live as a leper, as far away from the outside world as possible."

Chiun said, "It is a sad story. But how did you come to leave Molokai for this godforsaken place?"

"It was for Ana," the chief said. "You see, after her wounds were healed, Zoran continued to treat her in her mind."

"Hypnosis," Smith said. It was one of Lustbaden's specialties.

"He said it was to help her recover from the shock, but later Ana told me in private that he used the sessions to perform shameful acts on her."

Smith felt a wave of disgust. He remembered Dimi's beautiful daughter, used by Lustbaden until the day she killed herself with a broken bottle.

"But he had her *mind*," Timu cried out. "He had words that brought the rape on the road back to her. He had her trained to remember the pain and fear whenever she refused to do his will." He clasped Chiun's hand. "That was why I told your son not to befriend Ana. Zoran's power over her is such that she cannot even feel friendship toward another without reliving every terrible moment of that day on the road."

"Odd," was all Smith had to say.

"The villagers stay away from her. They must, although they love her as I do. Many have gone to their deaths for befriending Ana. The pain comes to her, and it controls her. Only Zoran can stop it then. She goes to him. Zoran has twisted her so that she belongs to him, not with her heart, but with the terror in her mind."

"I understand," Chiun said. "So when Zoran left Molokai, Ana had to go with him. But why did you and your people follow him also? You could have stayed in Hawaii, where you could live comfortably."

"He would not take her without us. He said she would suffer until she died of the pain. Fifty lepers of all ages, he demanded. It was up to me to convince them to come." He spoke to the ground. "My people were sold into slavery by their chief, because they trusted me."

Timu's face was streaked with silent tears. Smith cleared his throat.

"Zoran promised us the best care," the chief

went on. "Medicines, schools, hospitals, homes. I did not know it was all a lie. He said he would find a cure for us."

"What about Ana?" Chiun said. "She said he was a liar."

Timu hung his head. "Zoran is a man of strong will and polished words. He told me that Ana's accusations against him were false, that she was crazy. For a time I believed him. Or perhaps I only wanted to believe him, in order to save my sister.

"We came here by sea, in the hold of a fishing boat. It was a long journey. Zoran kept us alive with drugs from his clinic, but we were not permitted on the deck with him and the crew. The air was heavy and stinking. We were treated like cattle. The fifty chosen ones," he said with a bitter smile.

"You mentioned words," Smith said. "Words Zoran used to bring on your sister's attacks. Can you remember what they were?"

"Foreign words," the chief said dully.

The sound of a stifled sob very near the hut brought Smith to his feet.

Chiun looked out the small doorway. A flash of red cloth, a tan leg disappeared into the rain forest.

"What was that?" Smith asked.

"The girl, Ana. She heard us."

The chief placed his head in his hands. "She has gone to the waterfall," he said. "She seeks comfort there. If only she could come to us. But Ana must remain either alone at the waterfall, or out of her head in Zoran's cave."

Smith considered for a moment. "Is she familiar with the interior of the cave?" he asked.

"Completely. When Zoran has her in his power, she is permitted to walk freely in his domain."

"She's got to help us get inside," Smith said urgently to Chiun.

"I can get inside," Chiun said.

"I know," Smith said. "But we need her as a guide once we're in there. I wonder where Remo is."

"So do I," said Chiun. "He should have returned by now. Let us talk to the woman."

The two men left the hut, thanking Timu for his honesty. "Be careful, my friends," the chief said to their backs as they entered the steamy darkness of the jungle.

Chapter Twelve

Remo awoke in a drugged haze, his wrists and ankles bound to his cot by steel bonds. Slowly he began to indentify the din that had been throbbing through his sleep as the soundtrack of an old anti-American propaganda film projected on the darkened wall. It was idiotic military pap, running repeatedly.

In the cot next to his, a young man sat transfixed, his bleary eyes staring blankly at the vintage film.

"You Caan?" Remo shouted over the blare of the soundtrack.

The man didn't answer.

Blinking hard to clear his mind of the fuzziness brought on by the injection in his back, Remo snapped off all four bonds and reeled slowly to the projector. With a shaky two-finger thrust, he snapped the motor in two.

The sudden silence sounded like an angel chorus to Remo, but the other man continued to sit forward on his cot, staring fixedly at the blank wall in endless fascination.

"Are you Richard Caan, the pilot?"

The man turned his head so slowly that it looked as if the movement were guided by a run-down mechanism. His eyes wouldn't focus. "Lieutenant Junior Grade Richard A. Caan, U.S. Navy, 124258486," he mumbled, his lips dry and stringy with saliva.

"Jesus, what's that nut been doing to you?" Remo said, appalled by the man's condition.

"My mission is to fly the F-24 over New York City at the appointed time," he said mechanically. "My mission is . . ."

"New York?" Remo asked. Caan repeated his drill. "But why New York?"

"My service will help to nullify the Soviet-American bloc, which terminated the divinely appointed Third Reich," Caan droned. "Through my efforts, the glory of the Fuhrer and his legions will rise again. My instructions are—my mission is . . ." His face twisted with confusion. "New York City . . ."

"Christ, Wacky Street," Remo said, snapping the bonds from Caan's legs. He draped his arm around the pilot's shoulders and lifted him up. "C'mon, kid," he said. "We've got to get out of here."

The pilot flailed in alarm. "I can't leave," he said.

"Sure you can. Just hang on."

But Caan fought him with all his strength. "I was told not to leave! Zoran ordered me," he muttered through clenched teeth.

"Come on, screw Zoran," Remo objected. "Just look what he's done to you!"

Caan turned his vacant stare into Remo's face. "I am a Jew," he said matter-of-factly. "It is not my place to question my superiors."

Remo exhaled noisily. "Well, you're not staying here. You can go conscious or unconscious. Pick one."

Then Caan screamed, a blood-curdling shriek.

"Oh, balls," Remo said as the door flung open and four uniformed guards rushed into the room. "Get out of the way," he said to Caan, shoving the pilot into a corner.

He worked them all at once. One slashing hand went to a throat, dropping the soldier on the spot. At the same time, he sent a knee into another man's ribcage, embedding the bones deep in the man's lungs and heart. He smashed a temple with a fast three-finger attack, then flew feet first into the last soldier, collapsing his chest cavity. It was over in seconds. They had all died instantly.

He grabbed Caan by the scruff of his neck. "I don't want to have to carry you out of here," he said to the cringing pilot. "But if you pull that trick again, I'm going to have to. I've got an old man to check on, and then I'm coming back here, I don't want you around. People are going to get hurt."

"You're an American, aren't you?" Caan asked, squinting at the stranger who could fight better than any commando.

"Yes," Remo said. "And so are you. Try not to forget it next time, okay?"

"I am a Jew," he said quietly, as Remo led him into the maze of underground corridors.

A half-mile or more farther on, deep in the cave complex, the corridor—now little more than a narrow stone walkway—emptied into a massive hall.

The sight was incredible. The huge area, obviously once the main chamber of the cave, was filled with military machinery and soldiers. There were dozens of them, all in the nondescript uniforms he had seen before, but the men in the cave wore armbands bearing insignia of the red and black Nazi swastika.

The walls were hung with forty-foot portraits of long-dead leaders of the Third Reich. At the far end of the cave, draped in thick folds of black, stood an awesome painting of Adolf Hitler.

"Zoran's got a freaking *army*," Remo mused aloud.

For the first time since they left the room, Caan spoke. "I think there's a channel near here," he said. "I heard the guards talking about it. But we'll have to get there through the hall."

"We'll stay near the wall." Remo looked out. "I think I see it. About thirty feet to the left?"

Caan nodded.

"It's a clear run from here. Let's go." He sprinted out, supple as a cat. Caan followed.

All Remo could see of the channel was a cave opening, but it was exactly what Remo was looking for. It was a perfect hiding place, dark and unobstrusive. Remo darted in. "Hurry up," he whispered.

But Caan hung back at the mouth of the

opening, directly beneath the arc lights of the massive work chamber.

"Get in here, will you?"

"You are an American," Caan said glassily. He pressed a button on the wall, and a steel mesh screen crackling with electricity, slammed down between them.

Remo touched his hands to the mesh. The jolt threw him backward into the darkness.

"I could not let you undermine my mission," the pilot said without feeling, staring at Remo's astonished face peering at him from the blackness of his prison.

They faced each other that way for what seemed like an eternity. Then a group of soldiers came quietly for Caan and led him away. He never looked back.

Chapter Thirteen

Smith sat down creakily on a rock beside the lake at the base of the great waterfall. "Magnificent," he huffed, watching the thundering cascade through a film of sweat. "Just let me catch my breath."

"Wait here, Emperor. I will seek out the girl."

"What's that?" Smith pointed to a high, frail ledge jutting out over the crest of the fall. On it was a speck of red.

"It is Ana," Chiun said, puzzled.

She stood on the ledge for several seconds, her body rigid, her black hair swirling around her like smoke. Then, lifting her face to the sky, she stepped forward.

"Ana," Chiun called.

But the girl didn't stop. Her hands at her sides, she careened off the ledge like a wooden doll, falling end over end toward the rock-strewn waters below.

The instant that she dropped, before Smith's horrified eyes, Chiun was propelling himself

111

over the surface of the lake in a dive so shallow and swift that he appeared to be flying. He clambered up onto the tallest of the boulders at the bottom of the waterfall and waited for the young woman to finish her descent. At the moment when she would have smashed against the rocks, Chiun raised his arms, caught her by the base of her spine and the back of her neck, and carried her back to shore.

She was unconscious. Before she could come to, Smith had joined them, panting from the exertion of the climb.

"That was remarkable, Chiun," he said. "I had no idea—"

"Silence. Let her awaken peacefully." He touched the girl on a spot just below her collarbone.

Her eyes fluttered open. "You should not have saved me," she said.

"That was for me to decide," Chiun said gently.

"I have brought only sorrow and pain to those who love me. Even Remo. For his kindness to me, I have returned cruelty. Zoran will kill him now, surely."

"He's still alive," Smith said with relief.

"Zoran has locked him in a channel of the cave," she said. "I just came from there. He is sealed in by an electric fence and surrounded by Zoran's soldiers. He can never get out. I have killed him, as surely as if I held a knife to his throat myself."

She choked on her own sobs. "Let me die. Please, Master. Do not save me the next time."

Chiun spoke crisply. "It is not in my power to keep you from killing yourself if that is your wish. No one can judge the suffering in another's heart. But I tell you this: your death will do nothing to help your people now. It will ease your pain, perhaps, but no good will come of it."

"But I betrayed your own son!" she screamed.

Chiun dried her face with one long sleeve of his kimono. "If you wish to aid us, you will be much more help alive than dead."

The girl blushed. She looked first at Smith and then Chiun. "How can I help?" she asked softly.

"Lead us to him."

"Zoran will find you. He sees everything. You'll be killed, surely."

Chiun shrugged philosophically. "We must all enter the Void at our time," he said. "To fear death is to fear life."

Ana stared at the ground, ashamed. "Yes," she said. "It is life I have been fearing."

"No one need be another man's slave," Chiun said.

Ana didn't answer. Picking up a twig, she drew a diagram on the soft earth. "This is the layout of Zoran's cave," she said. She pointed out the wide mouth of the cave entrance leading deep underground to the Great Hall and to the small cave, like an appendix, where Remo was being held behind the electrified steel mesh.

"A few rooms are above ground. They are for Zoran's use. Some even have windows. But most are deep within the earth." She drew a wobbly

113

line leading from a spot in the Great hall near Remo's prison to the outside of the cave. "This is a secret route leading from below the roots of a tree into the Great Hall," she said. "It was dug by children. Even the strongest security measures cannot stop a curious child from finding a way into a forbidden place."

"It is ever thus," Chiun said.

As the girl had told them, there was a hollow beneath the roots of an immense yew tree near the edge of the rain forest, facing Zoran's high-domed cave.

"Now, Emperor," Chiun said in his most diplomatic manner. "If you will be so kind as to wait for us here—"

"I'm going in," Smith said.

"Ah . . ."

But Smith was already lowering himself under the tree's spreading roots, frowning as he squeezed into the narrow passage.

"Crazed," Chiun whispered to the girl. "I brought him along to drive the boat." He gestured for the girl to enter the hollow, then followed her to cover the rear.

The child-sized tunnel was twisting and convoluted, with sharp rocks jutting out at all angles. Chiun seethed with impatience as Smith led the way at a glacial pace.

"Could we possibly move faster, O glorious Emperor?" Chiun asked with forced cheerfulness fifty feet below the ground.

Smith grunted and continued to creep forward at his same scawling speed.

114

"Why me?" Chiun muttered in Korean, rolling his eyes in the darkness.

Smith was running out of air. He had been belly-crawling through the barely passable tunnel for twenty minutes or more, and his nose and lungs were filling with loose dirt. There seemed to be no end in sight. No light, no space to breathe, nowhere to go but down, deeper into the airless earth.

He felt himself reeling. His elbows gave out. The girl nudged him gently from behind. "Are you all right?" she asked.

In the utter blackness of the tunnel, Smith recalled the grainy photograph of Zoran Lustbaden, with its cold, translucent eyes and lips twitching in a half-moon smile. He propped himself up again.

He had chased Lustbaden for thirty-six years. He would not allow himself to die now that he was so close to the end of the hunt. Keeping the image of the young doctor in front of him, he pulled himself painfully ahead.

Then, without warning, the ground gave way beneath him, and Smith tumbled with a wrench of his back into what felt like a deep, wide hole. He stood up as quickly as he could and held out his arms for the girl.

"Watch it, Chiun," he whispered when Ana was safely to the ground.

Chiun slapped Smith's outstretched hands away. "Do I not have eyes?" he said irritably.

"Well, *I* didn't see the drop," Smith said.

Chiun snorted in reply.

The bubble of earth they were standing in led to a curving passage. This one was taller than the narrow tunnel where they had crawled for so long. Smith followed the curve around a long S, then stopped short.

He saw light.

"The Hall," the girl said.

His heart thudding, Smith scrambled to the jagged entrance, keeping close to the wall. From well within the shadows, he took in the great portraits of Hitler and his generals, and below them, the orderly formations of Lustbaden's secret army, the SPIDER corps.

Someone shouted an order. Smith threw himself against the wall, but he had not been spotted. The soldiers marched away from the center of the Hall and stood at attention, waiting for some unseen presence.

Then it appeared. The F-24, majestic and silent, rolled through the Great Hall toward the main exit from the cave as Lustbaden's soldiers acknowledged it with a stiff-armed Nazi salute.

Smith felt himself being dragged back into the past—Warsaw, Dimi, Auschwitz . . . With one salute, all the buried terrors of a terror-filled war uncovered themselves and hurtled despairingly into the present.

"Good God," he whispered as the plane rolled past. And then one of the soldiers saw him.

The rest happened so fast that Smith saw it only as a disconnected series of events. A sudden rush of uniformed men, the girl's harsh, high scream, bodies flying like pieces of shrapnel as Chiun began his defense against the attackers. Then a cold blade whistled in the air and pressed against Smith's throat so tightly that he gagged. He felt the cut from the small motion of his throat reflexes.

"If you move, old one, your friend is a dead man," came a softly accented voice out of the chaos.

Chiun's arms dropped.

Don't stop, Smith tried to say, but no sound would come. Chiun looked back at Smith as he was led into the electrified mesh prison, where Remo's face was barely visible. The old Oriental's eyes, which usually showed nothing, held a look of deep alarm. With slow recognition, Smith realized that the spreading pool of warmth on his chest, invisible to him below the soldier's knife, was probably his own blood.

Out of the corner of his eye, he saw a stocky man with white hair walk leisurely past the group of soldiers. The man stopped in front of Smith and faced him. He tapped once on the knife at Smith's throat. "Very sharp," he said, smiling with his half-moon lips.

Thirty-six years.

Lustbaden clasped his hands behind his back and paced for several minutes, his eyes never leaving Smith's face. The doctor frowned, shook his head, chuckled, and then laughed aloud, his belly jiggling with mirth. "Well, well, Smith. We meet at last," he said. "My men spotted you as soon as you reached the shores of our lovely island. We've watched you every step of the way. It's Colonel Smith, isn't it? Or have you been promoted?"

Thirty-six years of a chase that always ended with the quarry's disappearance. Thirty-six years of hunting a ghost. There had been times when Smith himself wondered if Lustbaden were real. But he was real; he was alive; the hunt was ended.

Smith felt a perverse kind of relief in watching Lustbaden crow over his capture. For he had seen the face of his elusive enemy, and even if this was to be the last sight of Smith's lifetime, he was grateful to have it.

He had found the Prince of Hell.

"Oh, you tracked me well. Kept me on my toes, so to speak. Buenos Aires was a close one. And persistent!" Lustbaden threw up his arms in mock frustration. "But you should have given up while you could," he said quietly. "Because in the end, you see, the OSS, the CIA, and even Harold W. Smith himself are no match for SPIDER. Or for me."

"No!" the girl screamed, struggling in the arms of two soldiers who held her. "You won't kill anymore! My people will stop you. We'll kill you first, you and all your trained monsters—"

"*Nie wieder!*" Lustbaden shouted, and the girl collapsed in pained shrieks and convulsions.

Lustbaden flicked his hand lazily at the girl. The soldiers dragged her away.

"And now, if you'll come with me, please," Zoran said equably to Smith. "I have rather a special welcome in store for you."

From their place in the cave behind the electric mesh, Remo and Chiun watched Smith, covered with blood, being led out of the Great Hall, past the pile of bodies Chiun had left behind. The soldier holding the knife at Smith's throat kicked him in the backs of his ankles to speed him along. Smith stumbled. He never uttered a word.

Chapter Fourteen

Smith's welcome took place on the operating table of Zoran's laboratory. In The Room.

"Tsk, tsk, a nasty cut," Lustbaden said, probing at the knife wound on Smith's neck. "But superficial. I'll take care of it immediately."

"Don't bother," Smith croaked in a gush of blood.

"Please. I insist." From a drawer he scooped up a handful of sparkling white crystals. Smith felt the steel bands around his wrists and ankles bite into his skin as he tried to move. "Your young friend actually broke these bands," Lustbaden said, smiling. "A very strong fellow. But they've been repaired and reinforced. You'll stay snugly in place. Now hold still. This is the remedy." He brought his cupped hands close to Smith's neck.

"What's that?" Smith asked.

"An old cure for bleeding." He poured it onto the wound and packed it in. It burned like fire. "Salt."

Smith gulped and panted with the pain.

Lustbaden's dead-fish eyes took in the sight with sick satisfaction. "This is just the beginning, Harold," he said. "May I call you Harold?" He held a glinting surgical instrument to the light. It was a long, thin cylinder that drew to a sharp point at the end. "I feel we've known each other for such a long time that formalities are unnecessary. Don't you agree?"

"Of course," Smith said. "You know me and I know you. You are human slime. A fungus."

"Now, now, Harold. Don't feel that way about it."

"I feel nothing but contempt for you," he hissed, barely able to move his lips.

Lustbaden waved the silvered instrument in front of Smith. The half-moon smile was forming. "Do you know what this does?" He asked teasingly. "I'll give you a hint. It corrects ear ailments."

"Why don't you just kill me and get it over with?" Smith said.

The half-moon broke into a wide grin. "Ah, but my dear fellow, don't you see? I don't want to get it over with. I have lived in fear of you for nearly four decades. No, I will not kill you for a long, long time, and when I do, you will bless me on your knees for the gift of death."

"You will rot in hell first," Smith said.

"Only after you, Smith."

He poised the instrument near the side of Smith's head, then slowly screwed it into his ear. Smith screamed as his eardrum felt the blinding, searing pain of the knife.

"For you," Lustbaden spat. "For your country, using its wealth and power to ruin the greatest civilization in history. For the Russians, who helped you to defeat us."

He twisted inside the ear again. Smith lurched, turned his head, and vomited.

"Adolph Hitler nearly saved the world from the scum you defended," Lustbaden screeched, the vapid blue eyes ablaze with passion. "You destroyed it. You and the Soviet Union. You are the murderers, not me. You killed the possibility of a perfect world."

He drew back his hand and slashed Smith across the face with the instrument.

"But the Reich is stronger than you think," he said, inches from Smith's face. "We are everywhere, in every country. Do you know why I stole your precious F-24? Because when your president meets the Soviet premier, it will be your F-24 that smashes into the World Trade Center, killing them. Their end. And from it, a new beginning. We will join forces again, all of us kept alive through the years by SPIDER, and we will march into your two killer nations, sweeping your people away like the garbage they are."

The pain in his ear faded away as Smith thought of the secret American plane, evading its own radar defenses, and then blowing up the World Trade Center building. And it would work. No one could stop Lustbaden now. Then he felt salt being packed into the cut on his face, and he screamed. He did not know if he fainted.

Lustbaden droned on, but Smith no longer

heard him. Instead, behind his closed eyes, he saw Vermont in September, crackling with dry leaves whipped by the crisp wind, the air redolent with the fragrance of running sap, the high horsetail clouds signaling the winter to come.

He saw his wife, once again as delicate and pink-cheeked and proud as she was when she presented him with their daughter. The most beautiful child in the world, he'd thought back then, astonished that such a perfect creature could have come from him.

He thought of snow and cedarwood fires and the cloying taste of his wife's inedible fudge and his daughter's face the first time she wore makeup. He'd made her take it off, telling her it was unseemly and ridiculous. She'd cried, but did as he insisted. Only much later did Smith admit to himself that Beth had looked rather attractive.

Oh, to have a plate full of Irma's terrible fudge. Oh, for a chance to tell Beth how pretty she was.

He heard a click and opened his eyes. Lustbaden was gone. He breathed shallowly to lessen the throbbing pains in his ear and his face.

The spectre of CURE loomed inside him. It would all be gone soon, the computers' self-destruct mechanism activated by the president's voiced command once Smith's death was confirmed. CURE was airtight.

One night there would be a fire in the executive offices of Folcroft Sanitarium, contained by the solid asbestos lining in the walls and in the computer room, and the next day there would be no secret organization to fight crime in America. No one would know that CURE had ever existed, except for the President. And Remo and Chiun—if they lived.

That was another matter. Chiun was supposed to kill Remo in the event of CURE's destruction, but Smith knew better than to believe that would happen. If they survived Lustbaden, Chiun would be all right. He would go back to his Korean village and live out his life writing poetry and telling stories to children.

But Remo. Where did a young man with a body like a machine and no official existence go? Would he become a mercenary, marching in some foreign army to fight whomever he was told for no reason other than a regular paycheck? Would he join a circus or a carnival sideshow, demonstrating his freakish strength for giggling schoolgirls?

Or would Remo just drift like a lost helium balloon, coming to rest in the cobwebs of dusty alleys with the rest of the world's misfit, castoff inhabitants?

Remo. On the day of judgment, Remo Williams would be cited as Smith's greatest sin. He had been chosen almost at random to become CURE's enforcement arm, this young man with no appetite for killing, whose only wish was to live the normal life of a normal man.

CURE, through Smith, had rendered that simple wish impossible. It had stripped away his identity, his past, his dreams. It had been for the best possible cause. Still, Remo would never be normal again.

Is it right, Smith wondered, to change a man's destiny?

His thoughts made his head pound with the thrust of a thousand poisoned spikes. A fever was already setting in, and his sweat ran cold. The blood and vomit in his mouth tasted foul.

His left ear was probably gone for good. What would be next—his eyes? His limbs?

Oh, Beth. Oh, Remo.

So many regrets. It was the curse of middle-age, Smith supposed, to be old enough to have accumlated all of the questions of one's lifetime, and still too young to know any of the answers.

But there was so little time for regret now.

And so much pain.

With a great effort, Smith closed his eyes again and remembered Vermont. In September.

Chapter Fifteen

"A fine mess you've got us in now," Chiun said.

"If you can't be part of the solution," Remo said, "don't be part of the problem." He was on his hands and knees at the back wall of the cave, digging and probing with his fingers, trying to find a weak spot in the stone.

"My only part in this problem was ever having anything to do with you," Chiun said. "But my ancestors have punished me. Here I am, perhaps doomed to spend the rest of my life in a cage. With you. Watching you burrow in the ground like a mole."

"Quiet," barked one of the guards on the other side of the electrified fence.

Chiun responded with a babble of Korean.

Remo had found a small opening in the wall near the floor and, working quietly with his hand, chipped away some of the rock. He lay down, his face close to the rock floor of the cave, and looked inside the small hole he had made.

His pupils, already adjusted to nearly pitch-darkness, opened even wider to take in the greenish luminosity of the slime covering every inch of the tiny passageway.

Two dots of light, tinged with red, glowed briefly in the darkness. As Remo reached toward them, they disappeared with a scratching, scuffling sound.

He struck out his hand blindly and grabbed onto something warm and twitching that shrieked in the blackness.

A rat.

With a shiver of disgust he threw it away and heard it hit with a thud and a crackle of small bones.

Then he saw the lights again, redder this time, it seemed. But the two dots were joined by two others, and then four, and then hundreds more, piled behind and on top of one another, and they were coming closer, coming toward him. The opening behind the wall was not big enough for a man; only big enough for rats. Dozens of rats.

He recoiled. He had nothing to fight them with but his hands and his face.

He slapped at the ground, hoping to find a weapon. Anything—a hefty rock, a sliver of discarded wire from the mesh fence . . .

There was nothing. Only the slime-caked walls narrowing into obscurity and the menacing red eyes stalking closer. Suddenly, two rats darted toward him.

Remo drew his body back, away from the small hole he had made as the rats scurried by. Then, forcing every bit of strength he possessed into his hands, he slammed them against the cave wall.

The rock shuddered, chipped, and then bits of it tumbled down to close the hole. He hit the walls again, and the hole was filled over. Inside it, Remo could hear the squeaking of the rats, returned again to the darkness.

He stood up and walked back toward Chiun, wiping his hands on his black chino pants. The two rats that had fled around him now twitched, crusty and blackened, on the electric grating. As Remo looked past them into the Great Hall, the dim criss-cross pattern of light falling through the mesh netting dappled his face.

"The walls here too are useless," Chiun said, experimenting with his long fingernails on the wires that attached the grating to the side walls of the cave. "Perhaps with time . . ."

"There isn't time," Remo said angrily. He remembered seeing Smith, stumbling and grim, covered with blood, being led away by Zoran's soldiers. And he remembered the girl Ana's face, pleading with Zoran to stop his senseless killing . . . her pitiful threat to crush his army of trained soldiers with a village of dying lepers. He could hear her scream of pain as the Nazi doctor spat the strange command at her.

"What did Zoran say to make the girl lose her marbles the way she did?" Remo asked.

Chiun was flicking at the thin wires of mesh with his fingernails, making sparks fly with each small manipulation. "He said 'Nie wieder.'

130

The chief of the village talked of foreign words Zoran uses to bend the girl to his ways. But it was an odd phrase. In German it means 'never again.'"

"Never again?" Remo was stupefied. "*Never again?*"

"Yes. Why? Do those words have some special meaning for white men?"

"It's the motto of a Jewish group. *Never again.* They're talking about the Nazis killing six million people in World War Two. A strange thing for a Nazi to say."

He saw sparks flying out of Chiun's fingertips. "What in hell are you doing?" he asked, annoyed.

Chiun didn't look up. He worked busily with the electric netting, his fingernails tinkling against the sparking wires. "I am loosening the threads," he said.

Remo saw at once what he was trying to do. "I get it," he said. "Knock some of the ends off, hook them onto other loose ends, and boom, a short circuit."

"I am not concerned with circuses," Chiun said. "I wish only to stop the electricity."

"Sure, Chiun," Remo said, smiling.

"Ah, this will do." Careful not to expose his skin to the high-voltage mesh, he held up two frayed wire ends with his fingernails. "If this works, there should be a boom."

"The lights'll go out," Remo said.

"When that happens, break through the netting as soon as possible. We will use the darkness to get past the sentries and seek out Emperor Smith."

"I'm ready when you are."

As Remo got into position, Chiun brought the wires together. With a loud fizz and a light like the burst of a dynamite explosion, the electric portal blazed to life for an instant. Then it crashed into total darkness as the powerful lights in the cave gave out. A murmur rose from the soldiers.

"Now, Remo."

He thrust both hands through the netting and tore outward in a powerful breast stroke.

The stroke was never completed.

While Remo's hands were still clutching the mesh, the auxiliary generators of the cave were activated, and a pool of light from the Great Hall flooded into the dark prison.

The electricity entered Remo in waves. In an instant his feet were jolted off the floor. His hands , filled with live wire, smoldered and fried, unable to let go.

Then he was in the air, still shaking from the charge, thrust away from the electric wire by the tiny figure of Chiun, silhouetted in the spill-over light from the Hall.

He landed crouched on his feet and hands. The slime on the cave floor felt cool on his damaged skin. Even in the darkness he could make out the diamond pattern of the netting burned deeply into his palms.

Chiun lifted Remo's hands for a look. "These burns are serious," he said quietly. The old man sighed.

The two sentries outside the mesh doorway walked to the entrance and shone their flashlights on the crouching figures inside. They complained to each other as they examined the broken netting where Remo had nearly broken through to freedom.

One of the guards shook an index finger at the prisoners. "*Verboten!*" he said, pointing to the hole in the netting.

"Go suck a strudel," Remo said.

The soldiers shouted something else into the dark cave, then switched off their flashlights and stood guard over the entrance, their backs to the prisoners.

"I think I see a way out," Remo said, looking at his hands uncertainly.

"You are burned," Chiun said. "Even Shiva must give himself time to heal."

Remo looked askance at his old teacher. Chiun vacillated between calling Remo a hopeless white fool and insisting that he was the reincarnation of the ancient Eastern god of destruction. It was pointless to press him about it. All he would say was that Remo's unusual history had been written millennia before in the prophecies of Sinanju.

Remo didn't hold much with reincarnated gods. At the moment, a rock prison with an electric fence was the only reality he was concerned with.

"I don't know what Shiva would do, Little Father," he said kindly, "but Smitty's dying somewhere in this cave. We can't stay here and let that maniac Lustbaden kill him."

For a moment they stood facing one another in silence. "Very well. Do what you must," Chiun said finally. "But try not to touch the wires again."

"I might not have to."

He strode over to the mesh portal, purposely treading noisily toward the guards. "*Achtung!*" he shouted as he reached the circle of light.

The guard looked over with a start.

"*Warten auf ein augenblick,*" he said, summoning up all the German he knew. He beckoned the guards toward him.

They stared at him with dumb curiosity.

"*La via del tren subterraneo es peligrosa,*" he rumbled, reverting to the Spanish warning signs he had read on the New York subway. It wasn't German, but it would have to do. "*La plume de ma tante est sur le bureau de mon oncle,*" he whispered with a wink.

"Eh? *Was ist los?*" one of the guards asked, squinting as he drew near.

"*Auf wiedersehen,*" Remo said, thrusting his hands carefully through the tear in the wire mesh. He grabbed both soldiers by the collars of their uniforms. He pulled them toward the grating, then released them and stepped back.

They screamed when they hit the netting, and their feet bounced off the ground in a jerky tattoo. Their mouths opened, wide and contorted, as the cave plunged into darkness once again. A metal alarm, like the bells used at prizefights, sounded. In the blackness, the scuffling feet of the SPIDER corps took up their positions at the mouth of the jail.

Remo flew feet first through the netting, knocking down two soldiers on his way to the ground.

"Quickly, Little Father," he said as the orange darts of gunfire began to burst in the pitch-black cave.

But Chiun was already out. A heavy body whooshed upward, struck the ceiling with a loud snap, and dropped with a thud onto a group of soldiers. In the light of the gunfire, Remo watched the body twitching in a macabre dance of death from the hail of bullets pumping into it.

"*Herr Doktor!*" someone shouted as the barrel of a rifle grazed against Remo's neck in the confusion. He took hold of the weapon. With a backward kick he sent the soldier splattering against a wall, then swung the rifle in a wide arc at head range. A chorus of cracks, like splitting melons, rose around him, followed by the moans of the wounded.

"Let us go now and find Smith," Chiun said, and in the intermittent light of random bullets Remo caught a glimpse of his yellow robe fluttering in the distance.

Chapter Sixteen

Smith was alone in the laboratory, barely conscious. His breathing was labored, and he was covered with sweat. His eyes, for once unshielded by his steel-rimmed glasses, were bright and glazed with fever. Outside, running feet obeyed shrill commands, which grew louder as the soldiers closed in on the lab.

Remo looked around frantically. "There's a room with a window somewhere around here," he said.

Smith waved him away weakly. "Go," he rasped "Get Lustbaden. Have to stop that plane. Urgent. Too late for me. Go."

"Sorry, Smitty," Remo said. "You're coming along."

He snapped the steel bands from the table two at a time.

"He needs care," Chiun said, looking over Smith's wounds. "I will take him."

He lifted Smith off the table as easily as if the director of CURE were a stuffed doll.

137

"My glasses," Smith whispered, but Chiun was already carrying him through the doorway.

A stand of sentries heading down the corridor pointed at the old man and his bloody companion, with a confusion of gruff commands.

"Remo," Chiun shouted. "Stop these fools."

"No problem," Remo said. "Look for a room on the right with a window. It's got bars on it, but it's the only way I can think of to get out of here except through the main walkway."

"Stop chattering and fight," Chiun said as he ran with Smith down the long hallway.

Remo had been right about the room. The window sat high off the floor. Hoisting himself up with one hand while carrying Smith in the other, Chiun balanced himself and Smith on the thin window ledge while ripping out the bars.

From where he landed on the ground outside, he could see the main entrance to the cave, a gaping dark hole carved into the rock. Ahead, the paved airstrip, now cleared of foliage, stood out starkly against the jungle greenery. On the airstrip sat the empty F-24.

Smith was fighting for breath. There was no time for Chiun to waste with the airplane. He carried Smith to Timu who, with the other villagers, had gathered outside their huts to gape at the weird new jet.

"I require the use of your home," Chiun said.

The leper chief took one look at Smith's limp, blood- and sweat-soaked body, and bowed. "Please, Master. Use Ana's hut," he said. "I do not wish that your friend's open wounds attract the microbes of my sickness." He brought them quickly to the girl.

Ana was sitting in the dirt in front of her hut. Her eyes were glassy and insensate. Her arms hung at her sides as her fingers dug meaningless designs into the earth.

"Go in," Timu said. "I will protect you from those who seek you."

Chiun set Smith gently inside. He could tell by Smith's labored breathing that his condition was very bad. Smith was not a young man, and his physical resources had been squandered in his youth. There was little besides his will to live to fight death with.

Chiun placed his hand upon Smith's chest. "Hear me," he said quietly, but with the pointed intensity of a religious rite. "Your body wishes for death. It is weary and beaten. But your mind can stop it. The Void waits. Step away from that place, Smith. Will yourself enough life to heal. Will it, I say."

With that, Smith's body trembled like a feather in a windstorm.

"Breathe."

Beth. Beautiful Beth.

"Breathe."

Not the bottle no not the broken liquor bottle your wrists Beth, oh, the blood everywhere . . . No, Dimi it was your daughter who killed herself not mine I'm sorry I'm sorry I'm so happy it wasn't my Beth . . . Dimi, I'm sorry. . . .

Chiun lay his fingers on the sides of Smith's head, stilling the trembling. He felt a wash of despair course through him, and knew it had come from Smith.

"Good," he said. "Again. Breathe. It is another step back from the darkness. Take it. Breathe."

Smith exhaled deeply.

Timu brought a dipper of water into the hut. Chiun dribbled it carefully into Smith's mouth.

Smith's lips parted, and a stream of gibberish poured from his lips. It was all a confusion, full of names Chiun had never heard. His own name was mentioned, too, and Remo's. Smith called Remo's name often.

Then he lay still, and was quiet.

"You are safe here," Chiun said, not knowing whether Smith could still hear or not. "I must go gather some herbs for your healing. But I will return."

He left. The jungle was filled with the rare leaves and berries necessary to give Smith strength. When he returned, Ana still sat in the same position on the ground, staring vacantly.

"Is Ana ill?"

"In her mind," Timu said. "You know of her problem. She will recover." He bent down and stroked her hair. "Do your work, Master. No harm will come to my sister. Or to you."

"Thank you," Chiun said, bowing.

The sweet herbs filled the tiny hut with their fragrance. Patiently Chiun wrung poultices from cold water and placed them on Smith until his shivering stopped and his fever began to break.

His eyes flickered open. "Should have . . .

should have had him brought to trial. Lustbaden." He spoke quickly, with the urgency dying
men often express. "None of us would have to
be going . . . through this. . . ."

"Silence," Chiun said softly. "You are still in
grave danger."

Smith touched his ear, grimacing at the pain.
It was covered with wet, sweet-smelling silk.
Chiun's kimono sleeve was torn, and Smith
knew he had made the bandage with it. "Thank
you," he whispered.

Chiun nodded. "It is nothing."

Smith gasped for air. "Was it . . . nothing
. . . when you saved the girl . . . at the waterfall?

"Nothing," Chiun said, smiling.

"Remo?" Smith asked weakly.

Chiun's face was impassive. "He did not
come out from the cave."

It took Smith a long time before he could
gather the strength to speak again. "I changed
his destiny," he said.

Chiun looked at him with an odd compassion.
"No," he said. "You did not."

"CURE—"

"You do not understand the ways of Sinanju,
Emperor. This is his destiny."

Smith tried to clasp the old Oriental's hand,
but he was too weak to move. It was just as well,
he thought. It would only have embarrassed
them both.

He closed his eyes. It was snowing in Vermont, and Irma was burning fudge.

Chapter Seventeen

Smith knew that SPIDER had been in existence since the destruction of Nazi Germany, and its members had been sheltering its secrets since then, enjoying an invisible power around the world.

Smith knew SPIDER too well not to fear it. Remo did not.

So he had no reason to fear Wilhelm Wolfe that afternoon in the cave.

Chiun and Smith were out of sight. Remo stood alone in the cave's corridor, preventing the passage of Lustbaden's SPIDER corps until he was sure the other two men had escaped.

The soldiers halted to brace and prepare their weapons for firing.

"Come on, you goose-stepping bastards," Remo taunted.

A rumble passed through the troops as they separated to make way for a tall young officer with golden hair and shoes that gleamed with polish.

"Now, who the hell are you? The Student

Prince?" Remo asked belligerently, still carefully balanced for attack.

"I am Captain Wilhelm Wolfe." He spoke with the calm assurance of the well-bred and well-schooled.

Remo saw not that Wolfe's shoes were not just highly polished army issue, but handmade and of the finest leather. His uniform, too, made of superb wool, looked as if it had been specially tailored to his body's every contour.

"And you are our friend, Remo Williams?" he asked, drawing a manicured hand over his wavy blond hair. On his right ring finger, he wore an ornate gold ring embossed with the insignia of a spider.

"Two things," Remo said. "One, I'm not your friend and not bloody likely to be. Two, how'd you know my name?"

"Before, when the doctor gave you that injection, you spoke. You spoke of many things," Wolfe said affably.

"I doubt it," Remo said. "My body rejects poison."

"Yes, of course. The doctor noticed that. Only a few seconds after your injection, your body was expelling the poison from your system. It was necessary for Zoran to take extraordinary measures," Wolfe said.

"Like what?" asked Remo. He noticed that the soldiers behind Wolfe still had their guns leveled at him, and he moved closer so that Wolfe was in their line of fire.

"It was necessary for the doctor to give you four separate injections, directly into your ar-

144

teries and veins. That way, you could not reject the poison in your system without rejecting your blood itself. It was what kept you unconscious. And made you pliable. Clever, no?"

Now Remo understood why the drugs had affected him. But had he talked? Had he really told them about CURE? They knew his name. What else might he have said?

As if in answer to his unspoken question, Captain Wolfe said, "You told us a very great deal. Yes, we know who you work for."

"That's too bad," Remo said.

"Why?"

"Because it's your death warrant," Remo said.

"That is why I have these men behind me," Wolfe said. "To keep you from killing me. Oh, I have every confidence in your ability to do so. You broke the steel bands of the table in Dr. Lustbaden's laboratory. You killed a number of well-trained soldiers with only your hands. And you escaped from a high-voltage electric containment area, sustaining a shock that would have killed a herd of cattle. Yes, indeed, you are a most extraordinary fellow."

"Mail the citation to my house," Remo said. "I'm getting out of here."

"You may," said Wolfe. "Your friends have escaped."

"Good-bye," said Remo, heading for the room with the escape window.

"Except . . ." he heard Wolfe's voice say.

Remo turned. "Except what?"

"Except the girl. She is still here."

145

"Then I guess you'll just have to take me to her, won't you?" Remo said.

"If that is your desire," Wolfe said. "But there are things I must first explain to you."

He was trying to buy time, Remo knew. But why? To allow the F-24 to take off? But they could can that idea. Chiun was free now. With him and Smith outside, the F-24 had as much chance of getting to New York as a paper airplane.

Remo eyed him suspiciously. "Frankly, I'd rather kill you," he said, although he already knew he would not kill him, not until he heard the strange young man out. "All right. What do you want to talk about?"

Wolfe smiled. "Come with me."

His soldiers still stationed in position, Wolfe led Remo through the cave's labyrinth of corridors until they arrived at a door with a darkened pane at eye level.

"One-way glass," Wolfe said. "Take a look."

The room behind the door looked like a bachelor's apartment. A cluster of sofas, a small table, and a magazine rack were in the front of the room, near the door. Behind them stood a desk covered untidily by maps and flight manuals. On the wall was a large map of the United States, with a single red pin on a spot in lower Manhattan.

Beyond the room was more living space, but Remo couldn't see past the doorway, where a young man walked purposefully toward the desk, straightening his tie.

His back was to Remo. He was in uniform.

Remo watched him with mild curiosity as the man affixed a swastika armband to his sleeve. It was a routine motion, obviously one the soldier had performed many times. Then he turned and sat at the desk, unfolding one of the maps.

"It can't be," Remo said, his breath clouding on the glass as he strained for a better look.

There was no mistaking it. The Nazi soldier was Lieutenant Richard A. Caan, U.S. Navy.

"Quite an improvement, wouldn't you say?"

"Depends on how you look at things," Remo said. "His health seems a lot better from this morning, if that's what you mean."

"That is the point. Come. I want you to see something else."

They walked a few more yards down the corridor until they came to another door. Through the glass Remo could see a scarred old man, nearly Chiun's age and with only one leg, performing an astonishing series of rapid calisthenics. He looked strangely familiar, although Remo couldn't remember seeing anyone on the island in such superb condition, especially such an old man with a missing leg. . . .

"He's the one your men dragged away yesterday, isn't he?" Remo asked, no longer amazed at anything he would find in Dr. Zoran Lustbaden's cave.

Wolfe nodded. "Yes. During your dinner festivities. Now we can talk. Will you follow me?"

This time he took Remo into a narrow passageway.

"Look, you're wasting your time if you're

thinking of throwing me in the slammer again," Remo said.

"I wouldn't think of it."

The passageway led into a large chamber, plastered and curtained, even though it had no windows, to resemble a Victorian drawing room.

Two ornate stuffed chairs flanked a small, round table set with a tea samovar, two cups, and—strangely, Remo thought—an ornament of some kind. It was a transparent red glass ball with a wire filament inside.

"I see Herr Doktor has set out a toy to amuse us," Wolfe said jocularly, picking up the red ball. "He is very considerate that way. Look, this one has a mechanism."

He wound a small silver key at the base of the ornament, and the filament inside began to turn, glowing dimly, then brighter as it gathered speed. Within seconds sparks were flying from the filament, filling the red glass ball with magnificent, rhythmic fireworks.

"Amusing, yes? But I am sure a man such as yourself is not concerned with useless trinkets." Wolfe set the ball down on the silver tea tray in front of Remo. "Now, then."

The pattern of the tiny fireworks display became even more spectacular than it had been. With an effort, Remo tore his gaze from the ball and directed his attention to Wilhelm Wolfe.

"You have seen Lieutenant Caan and the old man down the hall. No doubt you will agree that, from a physical standpoint, their improvement has been quite radical."

"Radical," Remo said, blinking at the red sparks inside the glass ball.

"Zoran Lustbaden is responsible for that. His work with the birds has resulted in medical breakthroughs of the highest order. When the drugs he has developed are perfected, there will be no more sickness anywhere in the world. Just imagine it."

"If he's so good, why hasn't he helped the lepers?" Remo asked slowly, his eyes glued to the ball.

Wolfe gave a short, dismissive laugh. "Why prolong the lives of the unfit?" He shifted in his seat. "Besides, there are still some minor problems."

"Like what?"

Wolfe stared into a corner of the ceiling. "Unfortunately," he said, "the average human organism is unable to withstand the drugs themselves."

"You mean those guys we just saw . . . "

"The old man will die within the hour," Wolfe said.

"Hmmm," Remo said, entranced by the red ball in front of him. "Hey, why are you telling me this stuff, anyway?"

Wolfe leaned forward earnestly in his chair. "I want you to trust me," he said. "So I begin by trusting you."

"Makes sense, I guess," Remo said dreamily.

"Tea?" He offered a cup to Remo.

He waved it away. "Might poison me," He said, smacking his lips sleepily. "Not that I don't trust you, understand."

Wolfe laughed. "As you wish." He set the cup down. "But I would not poison you."

"Why not?"

"The doctor needs you. As I said, the old leper will die soon. Caan, who is stronger, will live considerably longer. Several days, perhaps."

"Just long enough to blow up New York City," Remo said, not particularly concerned about New York City, or the summit meeting, or the lives of the two heads of state that were about to be snuffed out. "That's the biz," he said.

"Indeed it is," Wolfe agreed. "You see that the effects of the drugs are dependent on the physical stamina of the user. Also, to some extent, on one's mental stability."

He sipped his tea gracefully. "The drugs sometimes trigger unusual mental fixations," he said off-handedly. "The old man's penchant for pushups, for example. We showed him how to perform one, and he's been at it for two days." He laughed heartily.

"What about Caan?" Remo asked.

"We were careful to fixate him on his mission. Nothing else is in his mind."

"How do you know?"

"Tests."

"Oh." Remo nodded, trying to look as if he weren't falling asleep. "What if he thinks about something else?"

Wolfe shrugged. "It would be disastrous for his concentration, I suppose. But that is hypothetical. He is interested in nothing besides his mission."

"Nothing?"

Wolfe shrugged. "On rare occasions he talks in his sleep. Speaks in German, of all things."

"What's he say?"

"Nothing important. He calls for his grand-mother. He repeats schoolbook German phrases. Has a terrible accent." His eyes sparkled with amusement.

Remo tried to shake away the sleep that was falling on him like a blanket. Why would Caan speak German in his sleep?

"Give me an example."

"Of what? His German?"

"What he talks about."

Wolfe pursed his lips, thinking. "Quite unin-teresting things, really. Thank you for your hos-pitality; where is the bathroom . . . things like that." He snapped his fingers. "Oh, yes. He also uses a phrase of Dr. Lustbaden's from time to time. *Nie wieder*. It means—"

"I know what it means. He used it with Ana. It's some kind of hypnotic trigger word."

Wolfe raised his eyebrows. "How very obser-vant," he said. He picked up the red glass ball and held it close to Remo's face.

Remo blinked twice, very slowly. "You're trying to hypnotize me, too, aren't you? I ought to warn you. I can't be drugged, and I can't be hypnotized."

"Of course you can't," Wolfe said. "Just re-lax."

151

The red ball seemed to grow before Remo's eyes, expanding to fill the room, the universe. "But Caan . . . "

"Don't concern yourself with Caan," Wolfe said quietly. "It is an ordinary thing. And it only happens in his sleep."

Remo sighed. "Okay," he said groggily.

Only in his sleep.

"So what about me?" he asked, feeling his eyes glaze over.

Wolfe smiled. "The doctor and I feel that your physical and mental control are so highly evolved that you could shift your concentration at will. The old man is good only for pushups. Caan, who is stronger, has been prepared for his mission. But *you*, Remo." He stretched out his arms. "With the doctor's help, you will be able to do anything."

"No kidding," Remo said.

Amost imperceptibly, Wolfe moved the sparkling red glass ball closer to Remo.

"If the doctor can use you for his studies, it will further the cause of mankind by a thousand years. He will create with you a true *Ubermensch*, a superman whose seed will spawn a new generation of superior beings."

Remo grinned.

"So you see, we will make every effort to keep you alive, both now and later—after the incident in New York."

"Caan's going to blow up the summit meeting," Remo said, confused. He knew it was important to remember that the president and the

Soviet premier were going to be murdered by Kamikaze attack. But he couldn't for the life of him figure out why.

"It will be a great beginning," Wolfe said. "The birth of the Fourth Reich."

"Is that like the Fourth of July?" Remo asked.

"Rather. Would you like to lie down?"

"Sleepy," Remo said.

"You'll find the sofa quite comfortable." He helped Remo up and directed him to a long velvet settee with a head cushion. He placed the red ball next to Remo's face. "How is that?"

Remo stared, smiling and transfixed, at the whirling lights in the ball. "Great," he said.

Almost as if it came in a dream, Remo heard footsteps entering the room and another voice speaking quietly.

"He is under control?" The voice asked.

"Perfectly, Herr Doktor."

"Well done, Wilhelm," Lustbaden said.

"He is an impossible subject," Wolfe said. "If it had not been for those time-released drugs you injected into his body earlier, he would not have . . ."

"I know," said Lustbaden. "That is why I injected them into his blood. Now we must simply keep him continuously drugged."

"Yes, sir."

"Our plan was good before," Lustbaden said. "Now it is perfect."

"As we expect of you, Herr Doktor," Wolfe said.

"First we destroy the summit conference and the rulers of America and Russia. And then we trot out this man as a secret weapon for a secret American agency and blame the disaster on him. Russia and America will be at war in hours. They will be destroyed in days."

"Brilliant, Doktor," said Wolfe.

"Of course," Lustbaden said.

Remo heard footsteps cross the room. He saw two white legs beneath a lab coat in front of him, and he followed them upward, past the portly belly to the pink face framed with white hair, the cold blue eyes watching him behind the gold-rimmed spectacles, the lips curved absently in a half-moon. "You are well, Mr. Williams?" Lustbaden asked.

"Okey dokey," Remo said.

"Good. Enjoy your rest. I will be with you shortly."

"Always got to wait in doctors' offices," Remo said. His eyelids felt like lead.

Lustbaden turned to Wolfe. "You will remain here. I must attend to the business at hand. Your men will come with me."

Wolfe saluted. The doctor left the room, his heels clicking sharply ahead of the heavy thud of marching footfalls as he headed down the corridor.

"One thing," Remo said groggily.

"Yes?"

"Where's Chiun? And Smith? They really escape?"

Wolfe hesitated. "For now," he said.

154

"Good." Remo smiled and settled into his pillow.

"But we've destroyed their boat," Wolfe explained. "We'll find them as soon as the launch is completed."

"Launch?"

"Lieutenant Caan is leaving on his mission now."

Remo frowned. "Mission? Oh," he said, deciding he was too tired to ask about it. "You bring Chiun and Smith here," he added. "We'll all spread our seed around the Fourth of July."

"Oh, they're both too old," Wolfe said, laughing at the outrageousness of the suggestion. "Why, one of them is not even white."

"No Chiun?" His eyes opened wide.

"Shhh. Sleep, Remo."

"Can't sleep. Tricked me. Going to kill Chiun."

"Sleep, Remo."

And against his will he slept, all of him except for a small spark deep within him. That small part of him, unmeasurable and inviolate, waited for a special call beyond time and space.

It waited for the Master of Sinanju.

Chapter Eighteen

"Heil Hitler!"

Richard Caan snapped to attention at the words, shooting his right arm out in salute.

Lustbaden circled him slowly, nodding with approval at Caan's crisp attire, his ramrod stance, his clear, blank eyes. "Do you understand your mission?" he barked.

"Yes, Herr Doktor."

"And you are prepared to carry it out to the letter?"

"Yes, Herr Doktor."

"The maps? Have you everything you need?"

"Everything, Herr Doktor."

"Any questions?"

"No, Herr Doktor."

Lustbaden smiled, the half-moon lips quivering with excitement. "Then we shall begin," he said with an air of triumphant finality. "Collect your materials. The F-24 is on the runway. You will have to warm up the engine."

Caan went to his desk, where his maps and navigational guides were stacked. He leafed through them to double-check. He was a machine now, the perfect instrument for his mission. He no longer resisted Lustbaden, and was no longer punished. His health had returned within a matter of hours, thanks to the doctor's miraculous injections. All the suffering in that small room, strapped to a bed that allowed him no sleep, with the constant din of the projector in his ears—all of the discomfort, torture, and unspeakable pain were for nothing. He had changed it all just by saying yes.

By going along.

He walked to the bedroom, where his flight bag waited, already packed, on the freshly made bed. He picked up the bag, set it down again, and then followed a strange impulse to lift the pillow on the bed to his face.

It crackled with new feathers. The linen was stiff and blue-white, like the pillowcases in his grandmother's house in Brooklyn, scented with strong soap and the outdoor air where she hung her wash on a line.

Why would he think of Brooklyn at a time like this, he wondered. Why remember the family dinners of brisket, when his grandmother would bring out the aromatic platter, her face flushed, and set it on her crocheted tablecloth?

He shook the thoughts away and threw down the pillow.

The lace of the tablecloth was starched stiff. His grandmother sat in a rocking chair, even at dinner.

He picked up the flight bag and went back to Lustbaden. Without a word, the doctor

158

opened the door, and they walked into the long corridor.

On the third day of Chanukah, when Richard was twelve years old, his grandmother had given him a silver Star of David on a chain. It had been just the two of them, sitting in Nana's darkened living room in front of her gas-fueled fireplace, so Nana had decided to teach him German. It was a hopeless experiment. Caan had never possessed a gift for languages. Still, he remembered the scene as vividly as if it had happened that very morning: little Richard, his hair combed back with water, sitting at his grandmother's feet, the silver Star of David sparkling in his hand. And Nana, her white hair glowing like a halo as she rocked back and forth, back and forth, repeating words in a strange, harsh language.

He didn't remember the words. All he recalled was the movement of her lips as she rocked, speaking in German, the words, the words . . .

What words?

"Is something the matter?" Lustbaden asked over his shoulder. He was standing several feet in front of Caan in the Great Hall. Caan realized with a start that he had stopped walking altogether.

He felt himself blushing from shame. "No, Herr Doktor."

"Move quickly, then. There is much to do."

"Yes, sir."

Two guards met them at the entrance to the cave and escorted them outside. Farther down the airstrip, gathered around the F-24, Lustbaden's full contingent of SPIDER corps soldiers stood at attention.

The lepers were milling around in their village, buzzing in a state of high excitement. Several of them were clustered around Ana's hut, where the chief stood at attention, making discouraging gestures at curious villagers who tried to peek inside the doorway.

Lustbaden looked over the tableau, his eyes narrowing. "Just a moment," he said, leaving Caan on the airstrip with the two guards as he hurried toward the commotion.

The lepers scattered when he approached the hut—all except for Ana, who sat motionless on the ground, and Timu. The chief stood tall and straight, his muscles taut, the veins in his neck throbbing, his nostrils flaring with suppressed fear.

"What are you hiding?" Lustbaden demanded abruptly.

Some of the lepers scurried into their homes. Others backed away, whispering among themselves. Lustbaden heard the word Zoran several times, spoken with the awe one attributes to a deity.

Timu crossed his arms silently over his chest and spread his feet to cover the entrance like some terrifying colossus.

"Move aside," Lustbaden said, and shoved Timu with all his strength. The chief didn't budge.

Lustbaden stepped back a pace, his anger evident. A hushed silence fell over the villagers.

The doctor recognized his advantage at once.

"I am Zoran who speaks," he intoned so that all the village could hear. "I command you to let me enter."

Timu turned slowly to face him. "I have made my pact with one greater than you," he said. "You may not enter."

At that, the village seemed to burst with uncontrollable excitement. Even Ana looked up, nonplused by her brother's blasphemy. "Timu," she said softly, her voice a warning.

"Begone, Zoran," the chief said. He turned away from the doctor, his face as implacable as a stone carving.

"You filthy leper," Lustbaden spat. "You disgusting, subhuman vermin. How dare you speak to me with such insolence!" He drew back his hand and slapped Timu across the face.

The chief moved with the blow. He righted himself. Then, facing Lustbaden, he shoved the doctor with both hands into the dirt.

The villagers gasped. Women cried out. Ana skittered to her feet, her face a mask of terror. Lustbaden rolled to a sitting position, not bothering to wipe the dust from his face and white coat. His eyes were metallic, sparkling with hate. The half-moon smile was turned downward in a sneer of raw ugliness.

"Kill him," he hissed.

The SPIDER corps was already running toward the village. The two guards with Caan were closer, already kneeling, cocking their pistols. Caan stood beside them, watching.

161

Lustbaden screamed the command. "Kill him!"

Two bullets fired. Two wounds burst upon Timu's chest like bright blossoms. The chief staggered and fell.

"Timu," Ana cried, rushing to hold her still-breathing brother in her arms. The chief let her embrace him. "Oh, Timu, why?" she sobbed, rocking him. "Why did you speak against Zoran?"

His lips moved with effort. "I pushed him," he said wonderingly, blood trickling from the corners of his mouth. "And he fell. Zoran is only a man, after all. Tell them . . . he is . . . only . . ."

He breathed once more, and then he died.

And the soldiers closed in.

Chapter Nineteen

Lustbaden stepped past Ana and the body of her brother and stormed into the flimsy thatch hut. Harold Smith was inside, alone and unconcious.

The doctor kicked him hard in his side. Smith moaned in pain and shock, coming to with a ragged gasp.

"Where is the other?" he demanded. "The old Chinese?"

Chiun had been back in the rain forest for some time, but Smith, still groggy, mumbled only, "Don't know what you're talking about."

Lustbaden kicked him again. Smith bit down on his own hand to keep from screaming. The doctor stepped out of the hut. "Caan!"

"Yes, Herr Doktor."

His grandmother's face in the gaslight, rocking, whispering, whispering the words . . .

"Go, damn you!"

Caan took a few hesitant steps toward the airstrip, his head reeling in confusion. The mission. New York. Nana's brisket. The president.

The Soviet premier. The starched lace table-cloth. The World Trade towers. The F-24. Nana's lips, moving, moving with the German words.

The two guards who had shot the leper chief took up their positions beside Caan. He stumbled toward the airstrip, choking with tears he could not understand.

"You remain here," Lustbaden called to the two guards. "The rest of you search the area for the old Chinese dwarf."

The soldiers hesitated. They were all staring behind Lustbaden. He turned to see Ana standing stock still behind him, her brother's knife poised in her hand.

She spoke softly, but with a fervor that made even the doctor stop cold in his tracks. "Monster," she said. "Murderer. You killed my brother with no more thought than you would have for swatting a fly."

"Put down the knife, Ana," the doctor said.

But she walked nearer, her eyes on Lustbaden's, the knife held ready for attack. "Murdering swine."

Behind her, the lepers muttered in agreement.

"Ana!"

"You are afraid to die. I can see it on your face. Zoran, the great, the wise, the magnificent. Zoran is nothing but a little man gone mad with power. But your power ends here, swine."

"Swine!" a voice called from the crowd of villagers.

He glared at the lepers, but Ana was coming

165

still closer at the same steady pace. "Put it down, Ana. I do not wish to kill you."

She laughed, hard and bitter. "No, I imagine you don't. Who else on this island is there for you to whore with? Only me, the weak one who does all the dirty things you desire so that I can stay alive and out of pain."

Caan, walking to the airstrip, turned around to listen to the girl. She looked like a sleepwalker, her black hair streaming behind her, her arms outstretched, her knuckles white where they gripped the knife.

"But I have learned one thing, Zoran," she said. "There are worse punishments than pain. There are some things that are worse even than painful death. I do not fear you now."

"*Nie wieder,*" Lustbaden shouted. The girl screamed. "*Nie wieder!*"

The knife quavered, but did not fall.

"*Nie wieder!*" Lustbaden roared.

"You do not control me," she said slowly, struggling to speak. Her body was trembling. Spittle gathered around her lips. She would not be able to withstand him much longer, she knew.

"*Nie wieder,*" he said again, teasingly this time, his half-moon smile returning. The girl doubled over in pain.

Caan stood, frightened, a chill like a razor running down his back. *Nie wieder. Nie wieder?*

"The plane, sir," a soldier said, tapping his arm.

He looked at the young man in bewilderment. "The plane? Yes, the plane," he said ambling off.

He didn't even see the lepers pick up their rocks and clods of earth and hurl them toward Lustbaden and his men.

"Ana is right," someone called. "There are worse things than death."

"You murdered our chief."

"Zoran is a liar and a killer!"

A stone struck Lustbaden on the shoulder. The villagers cheered in approval.

"Fire," he shouted to his troops. "Kill all of these diseased scum. They never deserved to live in the first place. Fire, I say!"

The shower of bullets sounded like thunder, punctuated by the screams of the wounded and dying. But the lepers refused to run. Watching their neighbors drop beside them, an unspoken bond seemed to rise among the survivors and command them to stay and fight the soldiers with whatever weapons they could find—to stand and die.

A young boy took Ana's arm and helped her to her feet. You are brave," he said gravely. "Fight with us now. Do not fear pain." He picked up Timu's knife and handed it to her. "This belongs to you now," he said, clasping her fingers over the hilt.

At the edge of the rain forest, Chiun dropped the bundle of herbs and leaves in his arms and ran for the melee. He could hardly believe his eyes. Timu, along with a score of villagers, lay dead by the hut. Lustbaden's SPIDER corps was picking off the unarmed lepers in a bloody massacre of the people his ancestor had sworn to defend.

With a high leap that made him seem to float in midair, he descended on the soldiers with the fury of a jungle cat. The Nazis fired randomly, but their weapons were of no use against this small old man who possessed the force of ten divisions. He traveled from one soldier to the next, shattering their pistols and rifles with quick, complex strokes of his hands.

The lepers fought with him, cheering each other on as the soldiers dropped beneath Chiun's killing blows. When at last the few who survived had dropped their weapons and fled, Chiun stopped.

"Who is named successor as chief?" he shouted to the throng of villagers.

The young man with Ana stepped forward. "I am, Master," he said.

"Henceforth, call no man Master," Chiun said. "You are evenly matched, now that the soldiers have been deprived of their guns. Lead your people into battle with these evil ones who run from you, and do not fail."

The boy brightened. "I will," he said. And with a cry he brought the lepers forward to fight.

Smith looked up from his straw mat in the hut, trying to mask the pain from Lustbaden's kicks to his ribs and back.

"Is Lustbaden alive?" he asked.

"Yes."

"Why did you stop?"

Chiun answered softly. "With my skills, I can bring safety to the lepers. But only they can win back the pride that Zoran and his men have taken from them."

He wrapped Smith's ribs. "I must leave again. There is something I need to attend to."

"Remo?" Smith asked.

"Remo."

Smith took hold of Chiun's sleeve. "He's dead, he said quietly. "The plane. Stop the plane."

"Remo first." Chiun left.

Behind the straw hut he knelt, his eyes half closed, his heartbeat slowed almost to coldness. He sent his mind ranging through space, seeking to connect with another beyond the hearing of every other being in the universe. Chiun signaled only one word: *Shiva*.

You are created Shiva, the destroyer, death, the shatterer of worlds, the dead night tiger made whole by the Master of Sinanju.

And in the cave, deep in hypnotic sleep, Remo stirred.

Chapter Twenty

The SPIDER corps was gone.

The bodies of their dead lay strewn in a mire of blood and mud extending from the village clearing to the edge of the rain forest. Lustbaden alone remained, crying out frantically to his lifeless protectors.

"Get up!" he commanded, kicking a fallen soldier where he lay. "This is insubordination. This is treachery." He shook the corpse of another. "Do not betray me!" he raged, his white coat now bloodsoaked and torn.

Led by Ana and the new chief, the lepers converged on him.

"He is mad," the boy said.

"He has always been mad," Ana answered, steadyng the knife in her grip. "And we were mad to listen to him."

Lustbaden turned, his eyes wild. "I am not mad," he shouted hoarsely. "I am the greatest medical mind the world has ever known. You dare to come to me like this, you foul creatures with blood on your hands?"

171

"We will welcome your blood on our hands," Ana said, swinging the knife high over her head.

Suddenly Lustbaden laughed, the high-pitched giggle of a girl. "You forget," he whispered, his madness darting like lights out of the blue eyes. "The birds."

He held up his left arm, showing the wristwatch with the ultrasonic alarm. "I'll call them," he threatened. "I'll call them and you'll all die. Every filthy, stinking last one of you."

"The birds," someone whispered.

"Zoran still has the birds."

"The birds will kill us."

The villagers began to disperse, crouching and fearful, seeking shelter in their huts. Their victory had vanished.

"Come back," Ana cried. "Can't you see? He would not release his birds. He is in the open with us. They would kill him, too."

"They won't kill me," Lustbaden said, his half-moon smile twitching. "Nothing can kill me." He pressed the button on his watch.

A high shriek like the wail of a ghoul pierced the air. In the distance, the dark shadow of a gull flapped toward them.

Remo awoke.

Wilhelm Wolfe, who sat beside him reading, looked up in surprise when Remo rose from the settee.

"Get out of my way," Remo said.

Wolfe attempted a smile, but it died on his

face. There was something in Remo's countenance that frightened him down to his bones.

He picked up the red glass ball, its sparks still swirling inside. Remo swatted it away, shattering it in the air.

"What—what's gone wrong?" Wolfe said, more to himself than to Remo. He barreled around the room, opening drawers, searching frantically for some kind of weapon. At last he found a small silver pistol on the corner of a desk. Whirling around, he fired at Remo without taking aim.

Remo dodged the bullet easily. It came to rest in the wall behind him. "I thought you weren't going to try to kill me," he said. "Just you and me and the doc, remember? The three musketeers, sowing my Aryan seed for the glory of the Eighty-eighth Reich or whatever the hell it is."

With a sliding jump that took him completely across the room, Remo was on him, and the pistol was flying, and Wolfe cried out in alarm.

"I was only following orders. That's all. I meant you no harm personally."

"That's the biz, sweetheart." He grasped him by the back of the neck.

"Wait," Wolfe gasped, his eyes bulging. "Please."

Remo loosened his hold.

"I know that I must die," he said. The marks on his neck from Remo's hands stood out, raw and mottled. "Perhaps in another time, in other circumstances, we could have been friends." He shrugged. "That is of no consequence now. All I ask is that I be permitted to take my own life."

Remo considered. "Why?"

"I was born to an ancient and noble house. Dishonor would fall on the shadows of my ancestors if I were to be killed by a man with no weapons other than his hands."

"How would you do it?"

Wolfe held up his signet ring with the embossed spider design on the front. "Poison. I have carried it for many years. It will be quick, I promise."

He flipped open the gold spider top and stood staring into the hollow ring for some moments.

Remo stepped forward. "Is it powder?" he asked, thinking afterward that his question must have sounded flip at such a moment.

"No," Wolfe said, smiling faintly. "Acid," He hurled his arm at Remo, sending the liquid shooting directly toward him.

Remo ducked quickly enough so that the acid missed his face, but he felt the burn of the droplets on his back and shoulders. The cloth of his T-shirt disintegrated in huge holes, uncovering deep red marks on his skin. By the time he could stand upright, Wolfe was halfway out the door.

Remo caught him before he had taken another step. "Ancient and noble house," he said. He took hold of Wolfe's hand with its spider ring still on it and pulled slowly toward Wolfe's face.

The Nazi was panting, his eyes darting frenetically around the silent cave halls. "Who are you?" he whispered.

Remo looked him dead in the face. "I am Shiva," he said. "My line is ancient, too." And with that, he pressed the ring into Wolfe's forehead until the skull cracked. When he was finished, Wolfe lay alone in the empty hallway, his brain oozing from the back of his head. His eyes were wide and staring. On his forehead was stamped the red silhouette of a spider.

Chapter Twenty-One

The sky was dark with the huge, low-flying shadows of the birds. The clearing, once filled with villagers, was empty except for the two figures of Ana and Lustbaden, standing among the dead.

Ana's face was expressionless. She dropped the knife from her hand. "You have won, Zoran," she said. "We will all die now. I did not think you had the courage to give up your own life in order to kill us."

Lustbaden laughed, convulsive and maniacal. "But don't you see?" he said, tittering. "I won't die." He pulled a small vial of liquid from the breast pocket of his lab coat. "They will not attack me with this. Only you will be killed. You and the rest of your leper friends."

Seeing the girl's shock, he waved the vial at her tantalizingly. "But before you go, Ana, I wish to tell you a story. It's about the incident at Molokai. Your violation, my dear girl. By the gang of strangers. Remember that?"

He waited for a reaction from her, but the

girl didn't move. He arched an eyebrow in mock commendation. "Better, Ana," he said. "There was a time the mere mention of it would have sent you into paroxysms."

"I no longer fear the past," she said.

"Good. Good, good, good. Because I wish to inform you, in the hour of your death, that the men who raped you were my men, SPIDER corps troops I had been gathering from all over Europe."

"What?" The color drained from her cheeks.

"I kept them on Molokai, outside the leper colony, where I knew the authorities wouldn't come. Through hypnosis, I trained your mind not to remember their faces. But they've been here with you all along, ever since that day in Hawaii." He laughed uproariously.

"But you—you found me," she stammered in a small voice.

"Naturally I found you," he said. "My darling, I was the first to have you."

She seemed to explode from within. "You!" she cried, picking up the knife at her feet and running toward him.

With remarkable deftness for a man his age, Lustbaden lunged forward and grasped her wrists. Then, with her hands struggling in his, he kicked her between her legs. The air whooshed out of her in a gust. She crumpled to the ground in a heap.

He unscrewed the lid to the glass vial. "Good-bye, Ana," he said quietly.

Suddenly a loud bang reverberated in the clearing. Lustbaden screamed, his face twisted

178

in amazement as he looked at his left hand, which had held the vial. In its place was a broken shard of glass embedded in a bloody mass of tissue and bone.

Through his blurred vision, he saw a wisp of smoke lingering in front of one of the huts in the village. A man leaned in the half-shadow of the doorway, a Nazi Luger smoking in his hand.

It was Harold Smith.

"*Nein!*" Lustbaden shrieked above the noise of the oncoming birds. "*Gott, nein!*" It was a cry of rage and despair, the helpless wail of a man defeated on the verge of triumph.

"I won't kill you," Smith said. His face was bathed in sweat, the muscles of his neck straining with each word. "The birds will do that."

Lustbaden searched the sky, as if he remembered the birds' presence for the first time. He waved his arms at the flying killers above. There were hundreds of them, a blizzard of white beasts, mindless and lusting after prey. Lustbaden's arms, the injured one shooting off jets of fresh blood, fell to his sides in dull resignation. He looked like an old, old man.

"Not the birds," he whimpered. "Please. Don't leave me to them. Use your gun. Shoot. Please, Smith."

Smith looked pityingly at him. Thirty-six years. He had spent more than half a lifetime chasing this old man who begged for death.

He raised the Luger. Death was bad enough. But death by the birds would be slow and painful and terrible.

Lustbaden stood before him, trembling as he

179

waited for the bullet. He covered his face with his bloody hands like a frightened child.

This was not the Prince of Hell, Smith thought. Like Zoran, the island deity, the mad genius of the war camps was just another disguise Lustbaden had donned to hide his insignificance.

Smith aimed. A shot in the head would be painless and swift. He squinted through the sight. His head was swirling again. At the end of the pistol's barrel he saw a face, Dimi's face.

There was Dimi, alone and white-haired, shuffling in his shabby room, remembering his wife and daughter and his twin boys. Had their deaths been painless, those children under Lustbaden's knife? Did the daughter, with her sea-green eyes, die easily when she tore the broken glass into her own arm? And what did Helena, the kindly wife who had given Smith soup and a blanket, feel when she was marched into the showers at Auschwitz and found a stone in place of soap?

Smith threw the gun to the ground. "No," he said. "I'm sorry for you. The end will be bad. But I owe a justice."

Lustbaden stood still for a moment, his shoulders slumped. His round face was streaked with blood. With a final glance at the sky, turbulent with the flapping of birds' wings, he tucked his exploded hand close to his chest and scrambled on his fat, short legs toward the rain forest, seeking shelter from the birds he knew would find him.

Smith went back into the hut and collapsed.

Before he lost consciousness, it occurred to him that the birds would be coming for him, too, and for Chiun who had saved his life. Remo was probably already dead. And the plane would take off as scheduled. It was a sorry end for all of them, perhaps for all the world. A sorry end, senseless and mad.

In the darkness of unconsciousness that slowly enveloped him, he saw himself, as if from a great distance. He was weeping—for Dimi, for his family, for Remo and Chiun. Even for Lustbaden, the Prince of Hell, who was, after all, no more than a fool cursing in the shadows. And for himself, too, for the man with no answers. He wept for them all.

Remo ran toward the clearing at top speed. Overhead, the birds shrieked menacingly. Ahead, he saw Ana, standing alone and oblivious to the danger in the sky. Her face was starkly white, and she stood as still as a corpse, her hands crossed in front of her chest, as if preparing herself for death.

He reached her just ahead of the birds and pushed her into the hut. As the gulls descended, Chiun appeared from behind the hut, pale and trembling from his trance.

"Help me, Chiun," Remo said.

The old man took his place beside him in silence. Together, they waited for the birds.

The creatures dived in squadrons of twenty or thirty, their screams tearing through the sky. They dropped toward the two men, their beaks

181

open, their talons unsheathed and poised like daggers.

Remo took the leader, snatching its claws and throwing the beast to the ground. But when the rest converged, he grabbed whatever he could in the snowy fluttering of wings. Sinewy necks, cold beneath their down, snapped in his fingers. The air was thick with their gamy smell. Remo felt a wave of nausea rise within him as the bodies of the birds mounted beside him, and he was puzzled that the killing of beasts seemed more like murder than the killing of men.

But these were not natural beasts. He could tell by their weight, by the uneven distribution of their masculature, that these animals had been bred to become the sharks of the air—hardy mechanisms of survival, genetically programmed to kill on command.

He was surrounded by hungry black eyes like buttons, seeking out his own eyes. Their yellow beaks jutted and stabbed, probing for his throat. Already his arms were cut and bruised from their attack, and the acid burns on his shoulders were torn open. He killed mechanically, thoughtlessly, discarding the limp flesh of the dead as he grappled with the living birds.

At last they thinned, and the sky showed blue again. A few escaped over the ocean, their shrill calls growing faint, until the clearing was silent.

The Valley of the Damned, Remo thought, looking over the bloodstained wasteland. Flies buzzed around the heads of the dead soldiers and lepers. The felled bodies of the birds lay in heaps over every inch of the clearing. The huts were closed and silent, their inhabitants hiding inside. The place was aptly named.

On the edge of the rain forest, Zoran Lustbaden's mangled body lay twisted and blood-drenched. His throat had been torn out by the birds, and two gaping holes where his eyes had been stared upward toward the afternoon sun.

"It is nearly finished," Chiun said wearily. A white feather dropped from his shoulder and fluttered onto Lustbaden's open palm.

There was not so much as a drop of blood on the old Oriental's robe. "Nearly?" Remo asked.

"The plane," Chiun said. "There is still time to stop it. It is the Emperor's wish."

In the distance, Remo heard the drone of the F-24's engine as it prepared for takeoff. "Oh, God, Caan, you crazy Jewish Nazi," Remo muttered as he headed for the airstrip.

He was too late. The stealth bomber, with its terrible cargo, was already taking off.

Chapter Twenty-Two

Caan adjusted the oxygen intake valve on his helmet. He would be flying high above radar range, and the air would be thin. He looked straight ahead, out to sea, as the F-24 taxied swiftly down the airstrip.

The mission, he said to himself. Don't think of anything except the mission.

What was the mission?

Caan thought it over. Ah, yes. Brisket. Brisket and a starched lace tablecloth and pillowcases that smelled of lye soap. Rocking chairs and a Star of David and his grandmother . . .

"The mission," he said aloud, reminding himself. The films. The doctor. *Heil* Hitler.

"*Don't forget, Richard. Never forget. Never . . .*" His grandmother rocking, saying the words, again and again. *Never forget. Nevernevernever.* The wrinkled mouth opening as she rocked, talking soundlessly, the unknown words forming, talking, *talking—*

"What are you saying? He screamed, so loud that his voice cracked. Then he gunned the throttle and he was airborne, leaving the hateful old windbag in the dust behind him.

Remo reached the plane in time to take hold of its landing gear. The sudden burst of speed as the bomber climbed into the sky nearly threw him off into space, but he managed to hold on until the gear retracted. As it moved into the plane's body, he swung himself to get a foothold on the left wing, then propelled his weight in an aerial arc to land upright.

The wind was monstrous. At takeoff speed, even the aerodynamically perfect wings of the F-24 shimmied with the pressure. Remo felt the flesh of his face pulled backward with the thrust.

Slowly he crawled along the wing, his hands flat against the metal. It would be just like walking down a wall, he told himself, one hand after the other, supported by the toeholds of his feet, using his shifting weight and the vacuum created in his palms to keep himself attached to the surface.

But he knew it wouldn't be the same. It wasn't a wall, it was the wing of a jet roaring toward the speed of sound. And, too, the burns on his hands from the electric mesh of the cave prison hadn't healed. Fluid seeped from the raw flesh.

The pain shot through him as he reached the window beside the pilot's seat. Caan's face was comical in it s undisguised astonishment, but he was a good pilot. The plane never wavered. Instead, in the middle of its climb, Caan rolled it over in an aerobatic somersault and then dove.

Remo saw the earth turn upside down, its horizon curved in an upturned smile beneath him. The muscles in his arms were straining to their limit now, and his hands felt as though they were on fire. He wouldn't be able to stop the plane, he knew. There was only one chance open for him, and it was a million-to-one chance at that.

Wilhelm Wolfe had disclosed a crack in Caan's perfect indoctrination. "It only happens in his sleep," he had said. That was enough. It would have to be. With the last of his strength, he loosened one hand and pounded on the window. Caan looked over, his face frozen in surprise, as his plane continued its dive, trying to shake Remo loose.

"*Nie wieder.*" Remo mouthed the words carefully. "Never again."

He watched the pilot's eyes flare in panic, his gaze darting around the cockpit as if seeking an escape. Then he turned away from Remo to face front. His hands shook like dry leaves, as he pulled the plane out of its plunge.

There was nothing more Remo could do. Releasing his one remaining handhold, he dropped the scant fifty feet into the sea.

She was back. Rocking, smelling of flour and sachet, the Star of David sending white light dancing on her face as she talked.

187

"Never forget, Richard. . . ."

"Get out!" he cried, pounding at the controls in front of him. The plane dipped and veered, but the vision remained, speaking, the mouth opening soundlessly to utter the words that remained locked in the past, never to surface. . . .

But the words did come. This time, when she spoke, he understood. He heard the words as clearly as he had on that night beside the gaslit fireplace when he was twelve years old.

She said, *"Nie wieder."* Never again.

The mission.

The president. The premier. New York City. The stealth bomber. The mission, the mission . . .

"Never again," he said aloud.

The plane swerved in a great circle in the blue coastal sky, its contrails billowing behind it like a ribbon of clouds. It whistled as it descended, sparks flying off its silver wings.

In the village far below, Chiun helped Smith limp into the clearing. "Behold," he said.

In the ocean, Remo turned onto his back to watch the spectacle of the pilot returning to the island. "'Attaboy, Caan," he cheered. "Bring it in, kid."

But Caan had no intention of landing. His ears were filled with the music of an old lady's words as she sat rocking in the gaslight.

"Never again," he whispered as he flew the jet at full airspeed into Zoran's secret cave.

It exploded with a force that shook the entire island, sending down a rain of rock and earth and fire.

"Jesus," Remo said, averting his face.

Within minutes the cave was gone, the plane was gone, and Caan's remains were scattered to the winds.

The Valley of the Damned lay in stillness once again.

Chapter Twenty-Three

Remo staggered into the hut exhausted and looking like a war casualty. Smith, his head and face patched with bandages, was sitting up, already penciling in notes on an old sheet of yellowed paper.

"Where'd you get the paper?" Remo asked.

"Ana. She left, by the way." He held the paper at arm's length and squinted to read his own writing without his glasses. "You'll have to find her."

"What for?"

Chiun, sitting quietly in the corner, motioned his head toward Smith and described a coil near his temple.

"She'll be a danger, I think," Smith went on. "You'll have to eliminate her."

His voice had the same lemony quality it had exhibited at Folcroft. His manner was crisp and businesslike. It was all too clear that his time spent in the valley had done nothing to soften him. "I'm arranging to have the villagers sent back to Molokai," he said. "I don't think any of them know enough about you or Chiun to make a case, and they'll be isolated in the colony. But the girl's healthy. With her brother gone, she's got no reason to stay with the lepers. Given what she knows, it will be too dangerous to have her walking around. She might go to the press, anything." He shook his head in a prim gesture, his pinched eyes never leaving the paper in his lap.

Remo shook his head. "You'll never change, will you, Smitty?"

The remark caught Smith off guard. Remo was right. He hadn't changed.

His eardrum was damaged and perhaps punctured, his throat was scarred, and he had aged enough in one day for a lifetime. But inside, in his secret thoughts, he was the same terrified man who had thrown up his arms in a silent plea to the wiry stranger on the fire escape in Warsaw so many years before.

He still had no answers.

His mortal enemy, his monumental obsession, had turned out to be a cowardly lunatic, unworthy even of a bullet to die by. A frightened old man.

So were they both, Smith thought, frightened old men.

There were no heroics left to him. That was as it should be, Smith decided. Let Remo, with his strength and youth, try to fight the world with his hands. It was his destiny.

But for Harold W. Smith, all that remained was a job to do, a job with no room for heroes and no answers for him.

"Do as I say," he snapped in his brittle twang. "Somebody has to do it."

He looked up. "Incidentally, it was reassuring to see you come out of the cave alive. Good . . . er, generally good work."

"Rat droppings," Remo muttered as he left the hut.

Ana was at the waterfall, where Remo knew she would be. She was sitting with her knees drawn up to her chest, her black hair swirling with the mist from the fall. In the half-light of the vanishing day, she looked like something out of a dream.

"Hello," she said.

"Hello." Remo sat down beside her.

"I want this to be as easy for you as I can make it," she said, not looking at him.

"What?"

"Killing me," she said. She laughed at Remo's look of surprise. "I'm not an idiot. I know you're some kind of special agent. You're too expert a killer to be an ordinary spy, or anything like that. My guess is that you and the old Master are a well-kept government secret. And Smith is a bureaucrat if I ever saw one."

"Close," Remo said uncomfortably.

"So?"

"So what?"

"Go ahead, Remo," she said gently. "I don't care what happens to me now. I'm not afraid." She looked out over the fall, waiting.

"Well, what if I don't kill you?" Remo said defensively. "What would you do then?"

She looked at him sadly. "Nothing. No plans. You wouldn't be sparing me for a life of glory." Then the sadness turned to anger. "Go on. Neither of us has anything to lose."

"How about the villagers? They've got something to lose."

She shrugged.

Remo stroked her hair. "Look, I know this has all been a rotten experience for you—"

"Don't analyze me!" she snapped. "Kill me, all right? Just do what you have to do, and go away."

"You're worse than Smith," he mumbled. "Hey, you really want me to kill you, don't you?"

"Yes!" she shouted. "I'm sick of death and disease and craziness." She buried her face in her arms. "Get it over with." Her shoulders trembled.

Remo put his arms around her. "What say you get some sleep," he said. "And when you wake up, then maybe you can think of a few things to do with your life."

"Like what," she said bitterly.

"Like going back to med school. You could really give these people a hand if you did."

Her eyes rimmed with tears. "They don't want me. I've brought them nothing but sadness and disgrace."

"I think you're wrong," he said gently. "They've saved your life more than once. Maybe you ought to return the favor."

Ana didn't answer.

"Smith's sending them back to Molokai, you

know. You could go back to school in Hawaii."

Her eyes flashed for an instant. "Is that true? How would we get there?"

Remo cocked his head. "Darn," he said. "I'm supposed to kill you, remember?"

"Oh."

"But I don't think anyone'll notice if you're on the plane."

She looked at him for a moment, then turned away. "I'm so confused," she said.

Remo brought his face near hers. "Let me explain," he said, pressing his lips on her mouth.

She pulled away from him. "Is this the easy way?"

"Easy for what?"

"The easy way to kill me." She touched her fingertips to his face. "I know this is too bold of me, but I've wanted to kiss you since I first saw you."

"The thought crossed my mind, too."

This time she searched him out with her lips. "Don't be afraid to do it if you have to," she said earnestly.

Remo smiled. "With pleasure."

Chapter Twenty-Four

On the shore of the island, Chiun helped Smith struggle into a dugout canoe given by one of the lepers.

His ear was still swathed in Chiun's silken bandage. He held it as he wobbled in the small craft. "I don't think this is leakproof," he said somberly.

"I shall see to your safe return, Emperor," Chiun said with a patient smile. Remo turned his back to keep his grin from showing.

"We have to travel over deep water in this, you know."

"Do not fear," Chiun said.

Smith wavered awkwardly in the canoe, then sat down with a crash. Chiun's robes billowed dramatically as he swayed on his toes to keep the vessel in balance.

"That does it," Smith said, watching the water splash around the sides of the canoe. "I'm calling the Coast Guard."

"How?" Remo asked. "Your portable phone's at the bottom of the ocean."

"Oh. Yes," Smith said. "Still, we'll need a bigger boat. There's only room for two in this thing."

Chiun looked the canoe over, appraising. "You are right," he said, folding his thin arms in front of him. Then, raising his index finger, he said, "Ah. There is a solution. Very easy. No problem whatever." He sat down in the canoe, a satisfied smile on his face.

"What's the solution?" Remo asked suspiciously from the shore.

"The only solution, O imperceptive one." He turned in an aside to Smith. "I am afraid, illustrious Emperor, that you will have to row, for I am an old man, and weary with the burden of my years."

"What solution?" Remo demanded.

Chiun looked up. "Why, you will have to swim back, of course," he said innocently.

"What?"

"You act as if I had asked you to swim the entire ocean. This is no more than an exercise."

"I don't need the exercise, Chiun."

"Did you stop the airplane?" Chiun shrieked.

"Aw, come on. It was already taking off when I—"

"You need the exercise," Chiun said. "Besides, you will enjoy the swim. There is a magnificent colony of tubeworms ten or twelve miles from here. Be sure not to miss it. Shall we go, Emperor?"

With a grunt, Smith took up the oars. "I hope you're not expecting me to row the whole way," he grumbled.

Chiun smiled benignly. "Just do your best, sire. I can ask for no more. To give you strength, I will recite some of the more beautiful verses of Ung, penned by the Master Wang himself. Good-bye, Remo."

"Good-bye, Remo," Remo mimicked as Chiun's Korean singsong faded out to sea. "Ingrates!"

Chiun sniffed. "Ingrates. He dares to call me an ingrate. Did I not point out to him where he might find the colony of tubeworms?"

Smith grunted. He did not like Chiun's complaints. Sometimes the poems were all right. If only they weren't in Korean.

Remo waited until the canoe with the two men was well out to sea. He could hear Chiun's voice across the clear water. He was declaiming an Ung poem, and Remo remembered it. It was about a bee who sees a flower open. It took four hours to recite, and if Chiun was interrupted during it, he insisted upon starting over from the beginning.

High on a cliff, beside the crest of the waterfall, Reno saw Ana silhouetted against the twilight sky. She moved her arms over the back of her head, so that her long hair rose and fell in a sensuous cascade. Her breasts were high and firm, her legs slender and strong. She saw Remo and waved and smiled.

To hell with the tubeworms, Remo thought as he headed up the hill leading to the cliffs.

Tomorrow was another day.